The Ghost at Dawn's House

The Ghost at Dawn's House

ANN M. MARTIN

SCHOLASTIC INC.

For Lou.

Copyright © 1988 by Ann M. Martin

This book was originally published in paperback by Scholastic Inc. in 1988.

ISBN 978-1-338-64226-1

10 9 8 7 6 5 4 3 2 1   20 21 22 23 24

Printed in the U.S.A. 40
This edition first printing 2020

Book design by Maeve Norton

CHAPTER 1

"Aughhh!"

"Hi! Hello!"

"Oh, wow! Look at your tan! That's disgusting!"

"Your hair, Dawn! It's even blonder than before!"

It was the first meeting of the Baby-sitters Club since Kristy, Claudia, Stacey, Mary Anne, and I (Dawn Schafer), had been separated. It had been our longest separation since the beginning of the club. Two whole weeks. And we'd been scattered from here, in Stoneybrook, Connecticut, all the way across the country to California.

Claudia Kishi and her family had taken a trip to a resort in New Hampshire. Mary Anne Spier and Stacey McGill had gotten jobs (through the Baby-sitters Club) as mother's helpers, and had gone to Sea City, a New Jersey beach, with the

Pike family. Poor Kristy Thomas hadn't gone anywhere. She'd stayed here.

I was the one who went to California. I went with my little brother, Jeff. Our parents got divorced last winter and Mom moved Jeff and me from nice, warm California to freezing cold, snowy Connecticut. (Well, it was cold and snowy when we moved here. Now it's August, and hot and humid.) Mom chose Stoneybrook because she grew up here, and her parents still live here. Anyway, it was sort of a messy divorce, and Jeff and I hadn't seen Dad in ages, so Mom arranged for us to spend the first two weeks in August with him.

We got to fly by ourselves and everything. Since we were traveling alone, we were given all sorts of special attention. One stewardess slipped us free headphones. We saw *European Vacation*, starring Chevy Chase. Jeff laughed so hard he nearly got sick, but he recovered in time for dinner and managed to collect extra desserts from all the people around us who didn't want theirs — five in all. (Ordinarily, we're really into health food, but Jeff goes sort of crazy over chocolate cake.) Next, Jeff collected all the packets of salt, pepper, nondairy creamer, instant coffee, sugar,

and Jiffee Towelettes he could find. He
them in a barf bag. The barf bag is now sitting
his bureau at home.

Anyway, you'd think the airplane was the
highlight of our trip, but of course it wasn't. What
came next was not just California, but two weeks
of Disneyland Daddy — you know, two weeks with
a guy who hasn't seen his kids in months and
feels *really* guilty. Guilty enough to take time off
from work and give them a whirlwind vacation
of beaches, amusement parks, shopping, dinners
in restaurants, movies, treats, surprises. . . . It was
spectacular — except for the fact that a Disneyland
Daddy doesn't feel like your father anymore. But
I guess he's better than no father at all.

However, California was over now, and I was
back. All the members of the Baby-sitters Club
were back. And we still had two glorious weeks
of summer vacation left before we began eighth
grade.

As usual, we gathered for our meeting in
Claudia's bedroom. Claudia is the vice president of the club and the only one of us who has
not just her own phone, but her own personal
phone number. She's even listed separately in the
Stoneybrook telephone directory as *Kishi, C.*

"Well, let's get down to business," said Kristy, our president. Kristy was the one who'd had the original idea to form the club.

The Baby-sitters Club is really more of a business than a club. The five of us meet three times a week at Claudia's. People call us when they need a sitter. They're willing to wait until our meetings to call, because they reach five of us at once, so they know they're practically guaranteed a sitter. No more calling all over town to track down someone available.

We're very official and responsible about running our club. This is mostly due to Kristy, even though she does get bossy about things every now and then. We keep a record book full of information — the phone numbers and addresses of our clients, an appointment calendar, and a list of our earnings. (We each get to keep whatever money we make, but Kristy always likes to know how the club is doing overall.) We also have a notebook, a sort of diary, in which we're supposed to write up every job we go on. Then we pass the book around so we can all read what's happening with our clients. It's very helpful. But sometimes it's a pain writing about the jobs. Not all of them are that interesting. Of course, there *was* the time Kristy ended up dog-sitting instead of baby-sitting. And the time Mary Anne was baby-sitting for a little kid who got really sick, and found out just how helpful the 911 number can be in a real emergency.

Kristy opened the record book to the appointment pages in case a phone call should come in.

She leaned back in the director's chair and crossed her arms. "I move that we start this meeting by discussing the baby-sitting experiences we've had over the last two weeks."

(We'd all done some sitting, even Claudia and I, who'd technically been on vacation.)

Claudia grinned. "I move that before we start talking, we have a little snack," she said.

Claudia, the junk-food addict, pulled a book off her shelf, opened it, and removed a bag of chocolate kisses. It was a hollow book! Claudia has candy and stuff hidden all over her room, but she'd never gone so far as to use a hollow book before!

"Where'd you get that?" I asked.

"I bought it at a flea market. Isn't it neat? I got this, too." Claudia held out her hand and showed us a ring with a fierce, green dragon's head on it. Claudia, who is Japanese, loves wild clothes and jewelry.

"Ahem," said Kristy impatiently.

Claudia hurriedly passed around the candy, which Stacey and I turned down. (Stacey's a diabetic — no sweets for her.) Then she replaced the kisses in the book and tossed a package of crackers to Stacey and me.

"Let's start with Mary Anne and Stacey," I suggested. "I bet they had the most interesting experiences."

Mary Anne and Stacey, by the way, are our secretary and treasurer. (In case you're wondering, I'm the official alternate officer. I take over the duties of anyone who has to miss a meeting.)

Mary Anne and Stacey looked at each other. They exchanged a grin.

"You start," they said at the same time. Then they laughed.

I couldn't help feeling just a teensy bit jealous. Mary Anne is my best friend in Stoneybrook. She was the one who introduced me to Kristy and the others and got me into the club. Of course, Mary Anne already had a best friend (Kristy), but she's kind of shy, and she's always been envious of Stacey, who's sophisticated and grown-up. Now it looked as if Mary Anne and Stacey shared something — something the rest of us weren't a part of.

"I'll start," Stacey said after a moment of giggling. "First of all," she began, crossing her long legs, "we had a great time. I like the Pikes — all of them — a lot." (There are eight kids in the Pike family.) "We did the usual beach stuff — swimming, sunning, miniature golf. Claire is *still* going through that silly stage. She calls everybody a silly-billy-goo-goo. Vanessa has decided she wants to be a poet, so she speaks in rhyme."

"Really?" I said. I couldn't help laughing.

"Yup. It's true. And Byron can swim, but he's afraid of the water. It turns out he has a lot of fears."

"The most important thing about the Pike kids," added Mary Anne, "is something that's going on between Nicky and the triplets." (Nicky is eight. The triplets — Byron, Adam, and Jordan — are ten.) "Nicky wants to play with his brothers, but they don't like to have him around. They say he's babyish. But if they won't play with him, that only leaves the girls, and Nicky says he doesn't like girls. So . . ."

"Trouble," I said, nodding. This was important, since I sit for the Pikes a lot.

"Now tell us about you, Dawn," said Stacey. "I've never been to California."

So I told them about Jeff and the trip and my Disneyland Daddy. "I only did a little baby-sitting," I added. "Twice I sat for the kids who'd been my favorites when I lived in California. They were our next-door neighbors. I mean, they are. I mean, they're still Dad's next-door neighbors. There are two kids, five and eight. And you won't believe what their names are. Clover and Daffodil."

"What?" screeched the others.

"Yeah. My dad says their parents were hippies in the sixties. Flower children, he calls them. I'm not sure what that means."

"It must mean you have to name your children after flowers!" Kristy hooted.

We all began to laugh.

"Anyway," I went on, "they remembered me, and we were really glad to see each other. They cried when I left. They thought I'd come back to California for good."

"Oh, that's sad," said Mary Anne. Mary Anne is probably the most sensitive one of all of us.

"Yeah," I said. "But I'm sure I'll see them again. The next time I visit my dad."

"What about you, Claud?" asked Stacey. "Who'd you sit for?"

"Mostly this little kid named Skip," replied Claudia. "He and his parents were at the resort the whole time we were. It was no big deal. I just took him wading and stuff. A couple of other kids, too."

"Well," said Kristy, "*I* had some interesting jobs while you guys were away."

"Oh, that's right!" I exclaimed, suddenly remembering. "You baby-sat for the Perkinses, didn't you?"

The Perkinses were special for two reasons. Not only were they new clients, but they had moved into Kristy's old house. Kristy lives across town now, which was part of the reason she'd stayed home the past two weeks while the rest of us were away.

You see, I'm not the only one with divorced parents. Kristy's parents are divorced, too, only they've been divorced a lot longer than mine have. Long enough for Kristy's mom to meet a new husband. And to get married again over the summer. Kristy was even in the wedding! And all the members of the Baby-sitters Club were guests. It was great.

But then Watson Brewer (that's Kristy's stepfather — he just happens to be a millionaire) moved Kristy, her mom, her big brothers Sam and Charlie, and her little brother David Michael, across town to live in his mansion with him. It seemed like a fairy tale to me, but it has caused some problems. For one thing, we miss having Kristy nearby. For another, we have to pay Charlie to drive Kristy to and from our club meetings. Plus, Kristy's mom wants Watson and *his* two kids and Kristy and her brothers to become a real family. So . . . no vacation for any of them. Just plenty of togetherness at the mansion.

However, it was fun to have a new family in the neighborhood. And the Perkinses have little kids, which is even better. Kristy had been the first to baby-sit for them. A sitting job right in her old house!

"It was weird," Kristy said. "There was my bedroom and my living room — with this strange furniture. I mean, you know, *different* furniture. But the girls are great. And Mrs. Perkins is nice, too. I didn't meet Mr. Perkins. The older girl, Myriah, is really smart. And she takes all kinds of lessons — ballet, tap dancing, swimming. And she's only five and a half. Gabbie is the little one. She's two and a half. She says cute things like 'Toshe me up.' That's something she invented. It means, 'Pick me up and give me a hug.' And she kept calling me by my whole name — 'Toshe me up, Kristy Thomas. . . . Want to see my room, Kristy Thomas?' I think you guys will like the Perkinses."

The phone rang then, and once it started, it kept on ringing. Everyone knew we were home from our vacations and back in business. Even Mrs. Perkins called. By the time our meeting was over, we all had jobs lined up.

I rode my bike back to my neighborhood, feeling great. There were new clients to meet, baby-sitting to do, and two weeks of summer left!

CHAPTER 2

It's amazing how different two people in the very same family can be. Take Jeff and me. We're pretty much alike, except for the obvious differences, such as that I'm a girl and he's a boy, and I'm thirteen and he's only going on ten. But then take Mom and me. (Or Mom and Jeff, for that matter.) I love my mother and we get along great, but she's kind of like Oscar Madison in *The Odd Couple* and I'm like Felix Unger. Mom's not a personal slob like Oscar is, but she's forgetful and absentminded, and our house is usually a mess — except for my room. My room is the calm eye in the center of a hurricane.

This is why I was not surprised to walk into my house after the Baby-sitters Club meeting and find a pair of hedgeclippers in the living room, a trail of popcorn from the front hall to the kitchen (that was Jeff's — he's not a slob, but he *is* a nine-year-old boy), and a lot of other things that were in places where they didn't belong.

The mess has only grown worse since my mom got a job. Believe me, Jeff and I are happy that Mom is working — because *she's* happy she's working, and when she's happy, we're happy. But it does have its disadvantages. For instance, Jeff and I are now in charge of making dinner on weeknights. At first we tried taking turns, but that didn't work out, since Jeff's idea of making dinner is getting a loaf of pumpernickel out of the bread drawer.

Plus, Mom is so busy with her job that she doesn't have time for anything else. And I don't mean housecleaning. I mean dating. In particular, dating Mary Anne's father. See, Mary Anne's mom died a long time ago, and after we moved here, my mother started seeing Mr. Spier. Mary Anne and I were so excited! We thought we were going to get to be step-sisters. But I don't think that will happen now.

"Hey, Jeff!" I yelled. "Help me with dinner! Mom'll be home soon."

No answer.

"Jeff!" I yelled upstairs.

Still no answer.

Maybe he was in the barn.

I went out the back door, ran across the yard, and shouted into the barn. "JEFF!".

Thunk. What was that?

I stood still and listened. I could hear little rustlings. Far away, thunder rumbled.

I shivered. I love our old house and the barn, but sometimes they give me the creeps. They were built in 1795, and there's just something spooky about a place that's been around that long. So many people have lived here. . . . Some of them have probably *died* here, too. Right in the house or the barn.

"Jeff?" I said again, but this time almost in a whisper.

"BOO!" A figure leaped into view in the haymow.

"Aughhhh!" I shrieked. "Jeff, you scared me to death!"

He climbed down the ladder to the ground. "Well, you scared *me*. You come screaming in here like some kind of I don't know what. You made me fall off the rope in the haymow."

"Oh, was that thud you?"

"Yeah. What'd you think it was — a ghost?"

"Course not," I replied, sorry he'd put the idea in my head. "Come on. We have to make dinner."

Jeff and I fixed a salad with cottage cheese, pineapple, peaches, and coconut topping, and heated up a vegetable casserole Mom had made over the weekend. Then we brewed some herbal tea. Kristy kids us, but Mom and Jeff and I really like health food. We ate health food in California, and I think that's something about us that won't change, no matter how long we live on the East Coast.

"Boy, it's hot," I said, pulling my long hair away from my sweaty neck.

"I know," replied Jeff. "Sticky. Let's eat outside, okay? I could set the picnic table."

"Good idea," I said. I handed him plates, napkins, forks, and glasses, and he went outside.

I stood in our old-fashioned kitchen and stirred the tea. Then I poured it into a pitcher and added ice.

Suddenly, the house seemed awfully . . . big. I heard a creak and looked over my shoulder. Nothing.

Describing the house as "big" was kind of funny, since it isn't. Big, I mean. Oh, it has plenty of rooms, but they're all kind of small. Mom explained to me that over the years, people have gotten taller. Back in 1795, I guess we were still on the short side. At any rate, not only are the rooms

15

in our house little and dark, but the doorways are low, and the steps in the staircase are low (and uneven). It's like a large, creepy dollhouse.

Since the house *is* so old, I have this theory that somewhere in it is a hidden passage. All old houses have them, don't they? Claudia, who loves mysteries, lent me a Nancy Drew book called *The Hidden Staircase*. On the cover, Nancy is pushing open a section of wall at the back of a closet and discovering a hidden staircase. I know there's a secret something somewhere in our house, too. I just *know* it.

"Dawn?"

I jumped a mile.

"Oh, Mom!" I said with a gasp. "You scared me."

"Sorry. I didn't mean to." She kissed my forehead.

"How was work?" I asked.

"Fine. Busy, though. I'm pooped."

"I hope you're hungry. Jeff and I have supper all ready. Jeff's setting the picnic table. It's so hot we thought we'd eat outdoors."

"Oh, that's fine."

Mom was looking more absentminded than usual. Sure enough, she took off her glasses and placed them carefully in an empty butter dish. I wonder if she does things like that at the office.

I checked her quickly to make sure she hadn't been wearing nonmatching earrings or something all day. Luckily, she looked fine.

Mom and Jeff and I ate our picnic supper in a breeze that kept blowing our napkins away. At least it was cool.

"You know," said Jeff, chewing with his mouth open as usual, "it's getting dark real early tonight."

"Well, it *is* almost September," Mom pointed out.

"But it's only a quarter to . . . Hey!" I exclaimed. A fat drop of water landed on the back of my hand. Another landed on my head. "Uh-oh, it's raining!"

"And it's going to pour!" cried Jeff.

The sky wasn't just dark, it was black with heavy clouds.

BLAM! Thunder crashed. I remembered the rumblings I'd heard earlier.

"Everybody inside," said Mom. "Let's see if we can get all this stuff into the kitchen in one trip."

It wasn't easy, but we managed it. Jeff was the last one in and he scooted through the back door just as a sheet of water came cascading down. Lightning streaked across the sky.

"Made it!" he exclaimed.

Later that night I settled into my bed with a library book. I'd had my name on the waiting list for that book for most of the summer. That was how popular it was. And no wonder everyone wanted to read it. It was called *Ghosts and Spooks, Chills and Thrills: Stories NOT to Be Read After Dark*. Well, it was after dark, but I'd taken the precaution of turning on every light in my bedroom. However, the storm was still raging outside. The wind was howling, the rain was pelting the windows, and the thunder came and went, sometimes crashing loudly, sometimes just sort of grumbling in the distance. The grumblings were scarier than the crashes. They sounded like warnings of worse things to come.

I was right in the middle of "The Hand of the Witch" when the lights flickered. They dimmed, went out for a second, then came back on.

My heart began to pound. Weren't there tricky spirits called poltergeists that could cause things like that?

My window began to rattle. I know the wind was blowing, but I'd never heard such a racket.

As soon as the rattling stopped, I heard a rat-a-tat-a-tat on the wall.

That did it.

"Eeee-iii!" I shrieked.

Mom was up the stairs and in my room in about two seconds. "Dawn! What's the matter?" she cried.

"Mom, the lights are flickering and something's rattling my window and tapping on the wall."

My mother took a look at the book lying open on my bed. "Dawn," she said, giving me a wry glance, "there is a terrific storm going on out there. I'm surprised the electricity hasn't gone off completely. And *all* the windows in this old house are rattling. Those must be twenty-five-mile-an-hour winds out there. Now which wall is the tapping coming from?"

I pointed to the wall between my room and Mom's.

"Old houses make noises as they settle," Mom told me decisively. She closed the ghost-story book and laid it on my nightstand. "Why don't you go to sleep now, honey? It's late." She gave me a kiss and turned out the lights as she left the room, closing the door behind her.

I got up and turned two of the lights back

on and opened the door a crack. *Sleep?* Was she kidding?

It was hours before I fell asleep. That was because I kept thinking I heard someone moaning. When I woke up the next morning, I still felt creepy.

CHAPTER 3

The storm ended temporarily, but the rain didn't. The next morning was dreary, humid, and very rainy. I baby-sat at the Barretts' and the three kids, Buddy, Suzi, and Marnie, started out sleepy and cranky, and slowly became wild and noisy. I was glad they only needed a sitter for the morning. Here's an example of why.

As I was leaving, I skidded a little on the wet grass, and Buddy shouted after me, "Have a nice *trip*. See ya next *fall*!" He laughed loudly.

Suzi, who's four, shrieked, "Bye, Dawny-Dawny! Snap, crackle, pop!"

Marnie, the baby, blew me a raspberry.

I have to admit, I was happy to get home. Jeff and I ate lunch. Then I went to my room. Another storm was brewing, and I was planning to read some more of the ghost stories and scare myself silly. But the sight of *The Hidden Staircase* on my bureau gave me an idea. It was the perfect day to search — *really* search — for a secret passage in the house. I'd looked a couple of times before, but never very carefully or for very long.

I picked up the phone in Mom's bedroom and called Mary Anne.

"Hi!" I said. "Want to come over? I have this great idea. I want to invite the whole club to my house and we'll search for a hidden passage."

"Ooh," said Mary Anne. "Scary. I'd love to."

"Do you think the others are free?"

"I know they are. I was looking at the appointment calendar during the meeting yesterday. We all had jobs this morning, and we're all free this afternoon. Stacey's mother can probably drive us over."

"Perfect!" I said. "Listen, can you call Kristy? I'll call Stacey and Claudia."

"No problem."

An hour later, the members of the Baby-sitters Club were sitting expectantly in my bedroom.

"Now, we have to be scientific about this," I told them.

"Scientific?" asked Kristy skeptically.

"Well, sort of. See, there are certain things to do." I read them the pages in *The Hidden Staircase* where Nancy is searching Riverview Manor. "You tap on walls —"

"Why?" asked Kristy.

"To listen for any hollow sounds. A hollow sound might mean an empty space on the other side of the wall."

"And," added Claudia, who'd read a lot more mysteries than I had, "you have to feel around for springs or catches. And shine a flashlight over the walls. It might show up a secret opening you wouldn't notice otherwise." Claudia's eyes were sparkling. "*How* old is this house again, Dawn?" she asked.

I told her.

"Wow. I'd say we have a pretty good chance of finding something."

The storm that had been brewing finally let loose then with a terrific crash of thunder that banged the shutters and rattled the windows.

Stacey let out a little gasp. Then she giggled. "We're creeping ourselves out, you know. This is just a silly storm."

"I know," said Mary Anne, "but it's fun to creep ourselves out. We should take advantage of this super-creepy weather."

"Right!" I said. I couldn't wait to start!

"How do we begin?" asked Stacey.

"Let's split up," I suggested.

"Split up?!" cried Mary Anne. "I'm not going anywhere alone!"

I could see her point. The house was dark and quiet. Outside, the rain was falling hard and the wind was howling. I happened to look out my window just in time to see a bolt of lightning crackle across the gray sky in a jagged streak.

I shivered.

"Well, we don't have to go alone," I said. "We can split up into teams, one with two people and the other with three."

Everyone agreed that that seemed safe.

"Kristy, why don't you and Stacey and Claudia take the first floor," I suggested, "and Mary Anne and I will look around up here."

"What about the basement and the attic?" asked Claudia.

We froze. They were bad enough on a nice, sunshiny day, but today . . .

"Maybe the five of us should search them together. Um, later," said Stacey.

"Or — or maybe not at all," I added.

"Why not?" asked Claudia. "Those would be great places for a secret passage."

"I know," I replied. "But, well, in this story I read — it was called 'Things Unseen' — this man moves into a really old house —"

"As old as this one?" whispered Mary Anne. A gust of wind blew the curtains against her face and she shrieked.

"Just about," I said, closing the window. "And he hears all these spooky noises coming from the basement, and it turns out that years ago, a crazy lady buried her —"

"Aughh! Stop!" cried Mary Anne. "I don't want to hear the end of this."

"I do," said Kristy. "Leave the room for a minute, Mary Anne."

"I'm not leaving the room. Not by myself!"

Stacey shuddered. "I'll go with you."

They went out into the hall while I finished the story. When our screaming died down, they returned.

"Listen," said Kristy, "Why don't you two scaredy-cats be a team, and Claudia and Dawn and I will be the other team?"

Stacey took offense. "Scaredy-cats?"

"And you can search downstairs," Kristy continued. "Jeff is there and the TV is on. It won't seem so spooky."

"I think that's a good idea," said Mary Anne hastily. "Come on. Let's go before they change their minds."

They clattered down the stairs.

"Let's search room by room," I suggested. "I can tap walls. Claudia, you feel around for hidden springs and buttons and stuff. Kristy, you shine my flashlight everywhere to see if, like, the outline of a door or something shows up."

Kristy raised her eyebrows. She was used to being in charge. But this was *my* house and *my* search, so I thought I was entitled to give out a few instructions.

We set to work. We searched Jeff's room first.

"Boy," said Kristy. "My brothers would kill me if I ever searched *their* rooms."

"Well, Jeff might kill me, too, if he knew what we were doing," I replied. "But it's not as if we're searching his *stuff*. We're just looking at his walls."

"Oh, hey!" cried Claudia. "We should be checking the floors for trapdoors, too."

"On the second floor?" asked Kristy.

"You never know," Claud said.

Tap, tap, tap. I tapped and rapped every inch of Jeff's walls, but they all sounded pretty much the same.

26

Claudia followed me around, poking and feeling along the walls.

And Kristy crawled everywhere with her flashlight. She found two *Space Creatures* comics under Jeff's bed, but no trapdoor. We worked without speaking for a long time, and the only sounds we heard were our rappings and tappings, the pounding rain, and an occasional ominous rumble of thunder.

We didn't really find anything. There was an area near Jeff's bureau where the molding looked different than on the other walls, but no matter how much we poked and prodded, we couldn't find anything suspicious.

"Let's look in my room next," I said.

We started over again. I rapped, Claudia poked, and Kristy shined the flashlight.

"Nothing here!" said Kristy.

"Wait, I'm not finished," I said. "I've only done three walls."

Rap, rap, rap, rap, thud.

We all looked at each other.

"Did you hear that?" I whispered.

It was a definite hollow sound.

I was standing by my bed, next to the wall that separates my room from Mom's room. There was all this fancy molding on the wall — one of my favorite things about the room — and Claudia immediately began running her fingers over it.

The three of us were expecting something to spring open or fly out at any moment, but not a thing happened.

"False alarm," said Claudia at last.

I knew she and Kristy felt as disappointed as I did.

"Hey, you guys," said Kristy, forcing a smile. "Let's show those two cowards downstairs how brave we are. Let's explore the attic."

"The attic?" I squeaked.

KER-RASH. A clap of thunder shook the house.

"I think that was a sign," I said. "A sign saying we'd be stupid to go in the attic."

"Oh, come on," said Kristy. "It's all this ghost stuff that's stupid."

Maybe to her. I couldn't stop thinking about "Things Unseen." Or another story I read where a man picks up a woman he finds hitchhiking one night. He decides to take her home, but when he gets to her house, she's disappeared — and the couple in the house say the woman was their daughter and had died ten years earlier.

Kristy grabbed my arm. "Come on."

I must have been crazy. I opened the door to

the attic. We were greeted by stale, musty air, and the sound of the rain on the roof. We started to tiptoe up the stairs. The light switch was at the top. Halfway up, the door slammed shut.

"Yikes!" I cried.

The three of us piled back down the steps.

"I hope the door didn't lock behind us!" I whispered. We were closed into total darkness.

I was reaching for the handle when the door began to open slowly, all by itself. We heard a low moan.

"Oh, no," I whimpered.

Then we heard a growl.

"You didn't get a dog, did you," said Kristy. It was a statement, not a question.

I shook my head, and looked at Kristy and Claudia with wide, terrified eyes.

Then the three of us let out eardrum-shattering screams.

"Gotcha!" Stacey and Mary Anne jumped out from behind the door. "Who are the scaredy-cats now?" asked Stacey.

"You guys nearly gave us heart attacks!" gasped Kristy.

Mary Anne and Stacey laughed hysterically. The three of us had to sit down to recover. We didn't think it was funny at all.

"Did you find anything?" I asked them, when I was able to speak.

They shook their heads. "But we haven't looked in the den yet," said Mary Anne.

We split up again. As soon as Stacey and Mary Anne were gone, I turned to the others and said, "This is war. We've *got* to get back at them."

"How?" asked Claudia.

"There's a heating vent in Mom's room that goes down to the den. I have an idea."

The three of us sat on the floor and crowded around the vent.

"Ow-oooh," I moaned into it.

Kristy and Claudia caught on immediately.

"Heeeelp meeee," wailed Kristy.

"Wheeeere aaaaaaam IIIIIII?" whispered Claudia.

Then we moaned some more. The howling wind helped us along.

"Shhh," I said. "Listen."

Downstairs we could hear Stacey and Mary Anne shrieking.

I looked at Kristy and Claudia. We began to giggle. Then we took up the moaning again.

"Woooo . . . Ow-ow-ooooh . . . Oooooo-eeeeee . . ."

And then I felt a hand on my shoulder. I dared to look around. The hand was *green*.

"Kristy," I whispered. "Claudia."

We all looked up.

We were gazing into the green face of a deformed, one-eyed monster.

"BOO! Scared you!"

It was Jeff in a Halloween costume.

"Aughh! Aughh! Aughh!"

Kristy and Claudia and I were screaming upstairs. Mary Anne and Stacey were screaming downstairs.

Jeff fell over laughing.

That was the end of our search for a secret passage. We didn't find a thing.

CHAPTER 4

Wednesday

I know Kristy said the Perkinses are nice, but I have to say, I really didn't want to baby-sit for them. I'm still mad (only a little) that they live next door instead of the Thomases. Looking out my bedroom window just isn't the same anymore. (I look into Myriah's room now, not Kristy's.) But what I didn't know this morning was that "different" could be fun, too.

I did sit for the Perkinses today and guess what — Kristy was right. Myriah and Gabbie are *great. And boy is there exciting news at the Perkins house! It sort of slipped out by accident while the girls were coloring.*

I think I understand how Mary Anne feels about the Thomases and the house next door. Replacements can be hard to adjust to. Even if they're better than the original thing, sometimes you don't like them (at first) just because they're different.

Whatever Mary Anne's feelings, though, she *had* agreed to baby-sit at the Perkins home, so she showed up at ten-thirty on the dot on Wednesday morning.

She felt funny ringing the doorbell and not going right on inside like she used to do. Instead, she had to stand and wait. She heard a dog barking and feet running — not as many feet as when the Thomases lived there, but several pairs.

When the door was opened, two blonde-haired, brown-eyed faces were peering up at her. Behind them was a woman who was struggling to hold back a huge black dog.

There were a couple of moments of confusion. "Chewy! Behave!" said the woman.

"That's Chewbacca, our dog," said the older of the two girls. "He's eight months old."

"I'm wearing Myriah's baldet shoes," announced the younger one, holding up her foot to show Mary Anne a pink ballet slipper.

Chewy struggled out of Mrs. Perkins' grip, lunged for the door, and jumped up, resting his front feet on the screen and grinning a happy doggie grin. In the process, he knocked the littler girl to the floor. She giggled and stood up unsteadily.

"Baldet shoes are slippery," she said.

Mrs. Perkins got Chewy under control and let him out in the backyard. Myriah let Mary Anne in.

"Well, you're Mary Anne, right?" said Mrs. Perkins as she returned.

Mary Anne nodded.

"I'm Mrs. Perkins," she went on. "And this is Myriah" (the older one) "and Gabbie." (The one wearing the "baldet" slippers.) "Girls, this is Mary Anne Spier."

Myriah smiled shyly at Mary Anne.

Gabbie smiled, too. "Hi, Mary Anne Spier," she said, and I remembered that Kristy had said Gabbie called her by her full name.

"I'm going to the doctor for a checkup," Mrs. Perkins told Mary Anne. "I have to run some errands, too. I should be back in about two hours. There are no special instructions, really. The girls will show you their playroom. And you can go outside, if you want." (The rain had miraculously stopped.) "Oh, one thing — leave Chewy in the yard. If you take a walk, don't try to bring him with you. He's a bit of a handful."

"*He'd* take *us* on a walk, instead!" said Myriah.

After Mrs. Perkins left, Mary Anne and the girls looked at each other. Sometimes a first baby-sitting job can be a little awkward, especially if you're on the shy side, like Mary Anne is.

But Myriah got things going. "Want to see our rooms?" she asked.

"Sure," replied Mary Anne.

"I have a doll," said Gabbie, skipping ahead.

"It's not really her doll," Myriah whispered confidentially to Mary Anne as they climbed the stairs. "It's mine, but I let her use it."

Mary Anne smiled.

"This is my room," said Myriah a few moments later. And Mary Anne found herself looking sadly around Kristy's old room. In place of her sports posters were animal pictures and a poster of a ballerina. In place of her desk was a doll-house. It wasn't the same at all.

"Hey, let's go downstairs again," said Mary Anne huskily. "I want to see your playroom."

Gabbie turned and raced downstairs.

Myriah and Mary Anne followed. When they reached the playroom, Gabbie was already there, rocking an old Cabbage Patch doll in her arms. "This is Cindy Jane, Mary Anne Spier," she said.

"Her name is really Caroline Eunice," Myriah whispered. "Oh! There's R.C.!" she exclaimed suddenly.

A brown tiger cat sauntered into the room.

"R.C. stands for Rat Catcher," Myriah announced, "but he doesn't catch *any*thing. He's too, too lazy. Aren't you, R.C.?"

"Aren't you, R.C.?" echoed Gabbie absent-mindedly, as R.C. flopped over on his side and fell asleep.

"Now don't say everything I say," Myriah admonished her sister. Once again she whispered to Mary Anne. "The Gabbers is going through a stage."

"The Gabbers?" said Mary Anne.

"Yeah. That's what Mom and Dad and I call her."

Gabbie tossed Cindy Jane/Caroline Eunice to the floor. "Let's color!" she said.

"Yeah!" agreed Myriah. "Let's color. You want to color, too, Mary Anne?"

"Color with us, Mary Anne Spier," said Gabbie.

Myriah and Gabbie settled themselves at a pink and white table with pictures of Barbie dolls all over it.

"We always color at our Barbie table," said Myriah.

Mary Anne squeezed into a little pink chair. She had to sit sideways at the table, since her knees wouldn't fit underneath it.

Myriah tore three pieces of paper off a pad of newsprint and passed them out. She set a box of crayons in the middle. "Now color, you guys," she said.

The three of them (even Mary Anne) got right to work. Both of the little girls sang to themselves as they colored. Myriah sang "Take Me Out to the Ball Game." Gabbie sang "Hush, Little Baby." Mary Anne raised her eyebrows. How had they memorized all the verses to those songs? Even Mary Anne didn't know them.

After a few minutes, Gabbie handed her picture to Mary Anne. It was a huge, jumbled scribble. "Look, Mary Anne Spier," she said.

"That's lovely!" Mary Anne exclaimed. She was about to ask, "What is it?" when she remembered something we Baby-sitters Club members had thought up. Instead of saying "What is it?" when we can't tell what a picture or an art project is, we say, "Tell me about it." That way, the kid doesn't *know* we can't tell, so his feelings aren't hurt, and he tells us what the picture is so we don't say anything dumb about it, like "I've never seen such a big elephant," when it turns out to be a picture of the kid's grandmother or something.

"Tell me about it," Mary Anne said to Gabbie.

"Okay. This is my mommy," said Gabbie, pointing, "and this is the baby growing in her tummy."

Once again, Mary Anne raised her eyebrows. She almost raised them right off her forehead. "The baby in her tummy?" she repeated. She glanced at Myriah.

"Yeah, we're having a baby," said Myriah nonchalantly. "Not for a long time, though. I hope I get a brother. We have enough girls around here. . . . R.C. is a girl," she added. "The only boys are Daddy and Chewy."

"Wow! That's exciting!" cried Mary Anne. Actually, she felt even more excited than she sounded, but she knows how sensitive little kids are about new babies. She didn't want Myriah and Gabbie to think that they weren't important, too.

Mary Anne wanted to ask a lot more questions, but she didn't dare. She also wanted to call the rest of us baby-sitters with the exciting news, but she didn't dare do that, either. She knew she'd have to wait.

"Do you two want to take a walk?" Mary Anne asked Myriah and Gabbie. "It's so pretty out. And yesterday was such an awful, rainy day. I'd like to go out."

"Okay," agreed the girls.

"Hey," said Mary Anne suddenly. "Do you know any other kids around here yet?"

"We know Kristy Thomas," said Myriah.

"Kristy Thomas," echoed Gabbie.

"Well," said Mary Anne, "I meant kids your age. Have you met Jamie Newton?"

"No," said Myriah.

"Or Nina and Eleanor Marshall?"

"No."

"Well, maybe you'd like to meet them. It would be fun to have friends around here, wouldn't it?"

"*Sure*," said Myriah.

"*Sure*," said Gabbie.

"And guess what — Jamie Newton has a baby,

just like you're going to have. Only she's not a newborn baby anymore. Her name is Lucy. Do you want to see her?"

"Yup," said Myriah.

"Yup," said Gabbie.

So Mary Anne walked the girls around the neighborhood. By the time Mrs. Perkins came home, Myriah and Gabbie had met Nina and Eleanor, Charlotte Johanssen, Mr. and Mrs. Goldman, Claudia's grandmother Mimi, and Jamie and Lucy Newton.

"Jamie has a new baby, just like we're going to have!" Myriah told her mother.

Mrs. Perkins glanced at Mary Anne.

"The news sort of slipped out," said Mary Anne. "I hope you don't mind." She showed Mrs. Perkins Gabbie's picture.

"I don't mind at all," said Mrs. Perkins with a smile. "I guess I just hadn't gotten around to mentioning it. But it's no secret." She paid Mary Anne and walked her to the front door.

"Are you going to come back again, Mary Anne?" asked Myriah. "I hope so, because I didn't get to show you all the stuff in my room yet. Or in my goofy sister's room."

Gabbie smiled charmingly at Mary Anne.

"Of course I'll come back," replied Mary Anne. "And I'll show you something special, too. Right now. If you go up to your bedroom and wait by the side window, you'll have a surprise in a few minutes."

Mary Anne said good-bye to the Perkinses and raced home. She flew up to her bedroom. Then she stood at her open window. There was Myriah in *her* window.

"Hi!" called Mary Anne. "We can see each other!"

"Hey!" said Myriah. "We can talk to each other, too!"

"This'll be our special secret, okay?"

"All right!" cried Myriah.

Mary Anne turned away. Having the Perkinses next door still wasn't the same as having Kristy there. But Mary Anne didn't feel sad about it anymore.

CHAPTER 5

"Bye, Jeff! I'm going over to the Pikes'!" I called. "I'll be back in a couple of hours. Call if you're going to go anywhere."

"I'm not moving!" he shouted back.

The weather was unbearably hot, even for Californians like us. It was almost a hundred degrees and humid. Our old house isn't really equipped for air-conditioning, but there is one unit in the den downstairs. Jeff had been closed in with it all morning. I think that if he could have, he would have sat *on* the air conditioner.

I'm sort of in charge of Jeff while Mom's at work, but I can go off and do things. Jeff is almost ten, and he's fairly responsible. All either of us really has to do is phone so that the other one always knows where he or she is. And Jeff isn't allowed to have friends over if I'm not at home.

I made my way sluggishly over to the Pikes'.

Mallory, the oldest Pike, met me at the front door. "Guess what?" she cried. "All of us kids are here and *I'm* going to be the second baby-sitter! It was my idea, and Mom said okay!"

"Hey, Mal, that's great!"

Mallory is eleven and has always been a big help with her younger brothers and sisters. Until now, though, when all eight kids needed looking after, Mrs. Pike would hire two sitters. Apparently, she'd decided that Mallory was old enough to be one of those sitters. That was fine with me. All of us baby-sitters like Mallory, and we've sometimes thought that one day she could join our club. She's younger than the rest of us, but she'd be really good.

"Hi, Dawn," Mrs. Pike greeted me. "Let's see. Mallory's going to sit with you today. I'm sure she's told you that."

"Yes," I said with a smile. I glanced at Mallory, who looked as if she wanted to dance around with excitement and pride, but was containing herself in the interest of appearing grown-up enough to baby-sit.

"The triplets are in their room, practically draped over the air conditioner," Mrs. Pike went on.

I laughed. "Jeff's doing the same thing at home."

"Vanessa, Margo, and Claire are out in the backyard, playing in the sprinkler. And Nicky is . . . well, I'm afraid he's not in a very good mood today. He's in the rec room, sulking."

"Uh-oh," I said. "That's too bad." I thought about what Stacey and Mary Anne had told us at the meeting the other day — that Nicky wants to play with the triplets, but they won't let him.

"He's having a tough time," said Mrs. Pike, lowering her voice, "but he has to learn to deal with this."

"Tell Dawn about the two-block rule," Mallory spoke up.

"Oh, yes," said Mrs. Pike. "You know how we feel about rules around here, except where safety is concerned." (There are almost *no* rules at the Pikes'.) "Well, Nicky's been complaining that we treat him like a baby, so we told him that he's allowed to go off on his own during the day, as long as he stays within two blocks of the house. Two blocks *is* a rule for him."

"Okay," I said.

"So if he disappears, don't panic."

I knew Mrs. Pike was thinking of the time I'd been baby-sitting at the Barretts' and Buddy

Barrett really *had* disappeared. We'd had to call the police and everything. So I was kind of touchy about little kids going off on their own. I appreciated Mrs. Pike's understanding that.

Mrs. Pike left a few minutes later.

Mallory looked at me expectantly. "Well?" she said. "What do we do first?"

"At your house," I replied, "I usually check on everybody, just to make sure they're all accounted for. So why don't you go keep an eye on the girls, and I'll look in on the boys. Then I'll come outside with you. Maybe I can talk Nicky into playing in the sprinkler."

"Don't count on it," said Mallory darkly.

"Well, we'll see."

I went to the triplets' room first. Their door was closed to keep the cold air in. I knocked on it.

"Yeah?" called one of the boys. I wasn't sure which one.

"It's Dawn. Can I come in?"

"Okay."

I opened the door. The shades were drawn and the room was as dark as a room could be at two o'clock in the afternoon. The air conditioner was going full-blast.

"What are you guys doing in the dark?" I asked.

45

"Playing with our glow-in-the-dark space creatures," whispered Byron.

"They're about to be attacked by the Wandering Frog People," added Jordan.

"Oh," I said. "Well, I just wanted you to know I'm —"

"*Shoof-shoof-shoof-shoof-BLAM!*" Adam shouted suddenly. He thumped a Frog Person down on one of the space creatures.

"— here," I finished. I closed the door and left. The boys barely noticed.

Time to check on Nicky. I ran downstairs to the rec room. There he was, sitting in a ratty old armchair. A book was in his hands, but he wasn't reading it.

"Hi, Nick-O," I said.

"Hi."

"What are you reading?"

"Nothing."

"You want me to read to you?"

"Nah."

"Why don't you go out in the backyard? The sprinkler's on. You'll be much cooler there than you are inside. It's stuffy in here."

"Are the girls still out there?"

"Yes."

"I'm *not* playing with the girls. I'm a boy. I'm supposed to play with the boys."

"Not necessarily," I told him.

"I want to play with the triplets!"

"Well, then, come on. Let's go ask them."

Nicky looked at me with a hesitant smile.

"Really?"

"Sure."

We were about halfway up the stairs when the triplets came stampeding out of their room. They were each wearing bathing trunks and carrying a towel.

"Dawn! Dawn!" cried Adam. "We're going swimming over at Joey's! We just called him. His mom said it was okay."

"She said we could bring a friend, too," Byron added.

"She *did*?" Nicky marveled. "Oh, boy! Thanks! I'll —"

But before he could finish, Jordan said, "We called your brother, Dawn. It's all right if Jeff comes, isn't it? We said we'd tell you where he's going to be."

"Yes," I said with a sigh. "It's okay. Thanks for asking him."

Nicky watched the triplets run out the front

door. He looked absolutely crushed. A few tears leaked out, which he tried to hide. After a few moments he said gruffly, "I'm going outside to play. *By-my-self.*" He yanked the front door open.

"Two-block rule," I called after him.

"I know, I know, I know."

Nicky had been gone for about five minutes when I began to feel really bad for him. I decided I should find him and talk to him. I went outside and shouted his name over and over, but he didn't (or wouldn't) answer.

At last, I called Mary Anne on the phone and explained the situation. "Could you come help Mallory so I can look for Nicky?" I asked her. "I'd really appreciate it. It would be a big favor."

Mary Anne arrived in a flash. I left her and Mallory playing barefoot in the wet backyard with the little Pike girls. Then I started my search for Nicky. A two-block limit, which works out to a four-block area, is bigger than you'd think. I walked all around, through the Prezziosos' backyard, around the Barretts' property, even around my own house, calling for Nicky, looking for possible hiding places — in bushes, up trees.

Nothing.

I kept telling myself there were an awful lot of places a boy could hide. And I remembered what

Mrs. Pike had said — not to panic. But I couldn't help feeling just a *little* panicky. Why couldn't I find him? Maybe he wasn't within two blocks after all. If he was, surely he'd hear me calling.

"Nicky! NICK-EEE!" I shouted.

"Yeah?"

He'd appeared out of nowhere, looking dirty and sweaty.

I jumped a mile. "Nicky!" I exclaimed, half angry, half relieved. "Where were you?"

"Somewhere cool," he replied smugly. "The triplets didn't want me to come swimming with them, but I cooled off anyway. I showed them *and* I followed the rule."

I shook my head. "Come on. Let's go back to your house. You can shower off under the sprinkler. . . . And don't scare me like that again!"

"Sorry," said Nicky. He smiled at me. I smiled back, glad the crisis was over, but thoroughly mystified.

CHAPTER 6

When I got home that afternoon, Jeff was still off swimming. I didn't like to admit it, but I was nervous about Nicky's disappearance. Things like that scare me to death. I'd never gotten over the time I couldn't find Buddy Barrett. Children *do* get kidnapped. And I'm afraid it's going to happen sometime while I'm baby-sitting. It's not impossible. In fact, it happens every day. You read about it in the papers or see it on the news. I heard that there are thousands and thousands of missing kids.

So could I help it if I panicked a little when I couldn't find Nicky?

I needed to relax. I took my library book out to the barn. Now, the barn is not the coolest place I can think of on a hot summer day — but it is the most relaxing. It's almost silent. There's not much in the barn that can make a sound, and the sounds outside are muffled.

Usually I climb up to the hayloft to find a comfortable spot to read, but heat rises, so there was no way I was going to be anywhere above ground on that day. I looked around for a place with enough light to read by. But instead I settled for a spot with a little dry hay scattered around that actually seemed cool.

I sat down, all prepared to open to "The Haunting of Weatherstaff Moor," but I had no sooner gotten into a comfortable position than I heard a crash.

The crash was *me*! I was falling.

I dropped down, down, like Alice through the rabbit hole.

"Help!" I cried.

Thump. I landed hard.

"Ow!"

I looked up. Although I'd only fallen about five feet, it felt like five thousand. I was in darkness, but above me I could see a square of light, and beyond that, the beams in the roof of the barn.

I stood up shakily.

I was in some kind of basement or tunnel. No wonder that spot I'd been sitting on had seemed cool. All that basement air was circulating underneath.

Wait a second. Barns don't have basements. Do they?

Maybe I was in — Nah. Impossible. Besides, what was I? Crazy? I was standing in a pitch-black hole. I had to get out.

I felt around gingerly. I was positive my fingers were going to touch spiders — fat, hairy spiders (possibly fat, hairy, *biting* spiders) — or slimy things.

But they didn't. Instead they touched a narrow wooden beam, and above that another, and another, and another. It was a ladder!

I climbed back into the barn and examined the top of the hole. I'd fallen through a trapdoor. It must not have been latched properly.

Okay, so in our barn was a trapdoor with a ladder leading down into . . .

I shrieked. I *had* found a secret passage! I really had! What else could it be?

I flew into our house, grabbed a flashlight out of a drawer in the kitchen, and flew back to the barn. I was feeling pretty brave, especially considering what a chicken I'd been about exploring the attic the other day. But that day had been dark and gloomy. It was hard to feel frightened with the sun shining so brightly. Besides, I'd found what I'd been searching for so desperately. How could I not explore my own personal secret passage?

I shined the light down the hole. There was the ladder I'd climbed up. I backed down it carefully, holding the flashlight in my left hand. When I reached the bottom, I examined the floor. It was hard-packed dirt. I shined the light around and saw that the passage veered off to the left — toward our house.

I began to walk. The passage sloped down slightly. I was moving through a tunnel of earth with a few support beams here and there. The only light was from my flashlight.

I edged forward for a good distance. I was moving slowly, and everything seemed sort of unreal. At long last, the passage began to slope upward.

I shivered. This was so exciting. If I were just a little older, I could be Nancy Drew. Wait until Claudia heard about this!

"Hey!" I exclaimed aloud. Ahead, my flashlight was shining on a dirt wall. After all this, had I come to a dead end?

No, the passage made a sharp right turn.

I rounded the corner — and drew in my breath.

I found myself facing a crude wooden staircase. My heart began to pound faster. I climbed the staircase slowly. Where was I? Somewhere inside our house? I felt like the mice in *The Tailor of Gloucester*, darting from house to house in their secret passageways.

At the top of the staircase the passage, which was now very narrow, and all wooden (I was sure, somehow, that I was between the walls of our house) took another turn, and then, a few feet beyond, really did come to a dead end. I began feeling the walls around me, and suddenly something made a loud clicking noise and the whole wall to my right swung away from me.

I gasped.

I was looking into my own bedroom!

I stepped inside. The wall that had swung open was the one with the fancy molding that had sounded hollow the other day. The end of the passage was between my room and Mom's.

I was startled but immediately decided I wanted to explore the passage again more carefully. So I left the secret door to my room open (just in case), and stepped back into the passage. This time I kept the flashlight trained on the floor.

I blew up little flurries of dust bunnies as I made my way back to the staircase, crept carefully down the steps (who knew how sturdy they were?), and was soon back in the dirt tunnel.

And that was where I found it — the metal button. It looked positively ancient. I'd never seen one like it. It was sort of squashed in the middle, but I could tell that a design like a shield had been stamped on it.

A few feet farther along I found something else I'd missed. A large tarnished buckle. It was too big for a belt buckle, and not quite the right shape. A shoe buckle? People hadn't worn buckles that size on their shoes since . . . the eighteen hundreds?

I felt a chill begin at the nape of my neck and creep down my back.

A key was the last thing I found. It certainly looked old — very long and narrow with a large ring to hold it by. How many years had the key been in the passage?

How many years had all the things been in the passage? More important *why* were they there? Maybe they were all that was left of someone who had died in the passage — or worse, someone who had been locked up there to die. Maybe the poor prisoner had been trying to escape using the key. But he hadn't made it and had died a lonely, bitter death.

I knew it. I just knew it: *Our house was haunted.* It was haunted by the ghost of the secret passage. No one was going to believe it, but it was true. I remembered the rapping noises I had heard the night of the storm. Now I knew what had really made them.

CHAPTER 7

Saturday

Thank you very much, Dawn.
Because of you, we've all got ghosts
on the brain. Even I do. How else can
you explain what happened when I
was baby-sitting for Karen, Andrew,
and David Michael last night?

Well, it was a kind of wild night —
we had another storm — but usually
Karen's stories about Morbidda
Destiny and old Ben Brewer don't
really frighten me. What with the
weather, though, and the gigantic
house, and especially your tales
about "things unseen," I guess
the last straw was one of Karen's

stories. So thanks a lot — for the most embarrassing moment of my life!

The nice weather didn't last very long. By Friday it was gloomy again, and that night, the skies let loose with a storm that my grandfather would have described as a "ripsnorter." I didn't know it then, but while Jeff and I were having a ghostly adventure in our old house, Kristy was having an adventure of her own in her new house.

Earlier that evening, she'd been left in charge of David Michael, and Karen and Andrew, who were visiting for the weekend. Her two older brothers were at a party, and her mom and stepfather had gone to the theater in Stamford.

When everyone had left, the sky had simply been dark and threatening. An hour later, rain was falling, the wind was howling, thunder was crashing, and lightning was flashing.

Inside, Kristy was trying to interest the kids in a game of Chutes and Ladders, but it wasn't easy. Every time a clap of thunder sounded, David Michael shrieked, Andrew leaped into Kristy's lap, Louie the collie jumped (and skidded on the game board), and Karen looked disgusted and called everybody nitwits.

After that had happened three times, Kristy suggested, "Let's read a book instead of playing Chutes and Ladders. What should we read?"

"*The Little Engine That Could*," said Andrew.

"*Fantastic Mr. Fox*," said David Michael.

"*Ramona and Her Father*," said Karen.

Kristy rolled her eyes. "How about —"

"How 'bout if I tell a story?" Karen interrupted.

Kristy paused. Karen's stories are notorious. She never means to frighten anyone or to cause any trouble, but she always manages to.

"Do you know any nice, happy stories?" asked Kristy hopefully.

Karen thought for a moment. "Nope," she said.

"I want to hear a scary story," said David Michael bravely.

"You do?" asked Kristy incredulously, as thunder crashed and her brother jumped a foot in the air.

"Um . . . yes," replied David Michael.

"Me, too," said Andrew, not to be outdone.

Kristy thought that all of this was a bad idea.

"Oh, we can tell scary stories any old time," she said. "Let's tell jokes instead. Knock, knock."

David Michael, Karen, and Andrew glanced at each other.

"I *said*, knock, knock," Kristy repeated.

David Michael heaved a great sigh. "Who's there?"

"Banana," said Kristy.

"Banana who?" asked David Michael.

"Knock, knock."

"Huh? Wait, you were supposed to tell the joke part then."

"Trust me," said Kristy. "This one's a little different."

"Oh, all right. Who's there?" asked David Michael.

"Banana."

"Banana who?"

"Knock, knock."

"Who's there?"

"Banana."

"Banana who?"

"Knock, knock."

"Who's there?" demanded David Michael.

"Orange."

"Orange who?"

"Orange you glad I didn't say 'banana'?" Kristy burst into giggles.

The three kids looked mystified.

"So," said Karen, "this is the tale of what made old Ben Brewer so weird."

Andrew and David Michael sat up straighter.

Kristy made a face and began to put the Chutes and Ladders game away. When she finished, she left the kids in the playroom, went downstairs, and straightened up the kitchen. She found a package of graham crackers in one of the cabinets, placed it on a tray with four glasses and a carton of milk, and took the tray upstairs to the playroom.

There she found Karen in the middle of her story.

"Ben Brewer had been sitting in his rocking chair by the fireplace in his bedroom for six hours. Just sitting. Outside, there was a big storm going on."

"Like this storm?" asked Andrew, wide-eyed.

"Yup," replied Karen. "And now . . ." (she lowered her voice dramatically) ". . . it was almost midnight."

"Oh, no!" yelped David Michael.

Karen nodded solemnly. "And you know what that means," she whispered.

Kristy joined the children on the floor. David Michael was leaning against an armchair. Andrew was sitting in the lap of a humungous stuffed panda bear. And Karen, in the center of the room, was also the center of attention. As storyteller, she'd put on a witch's hat and a sparkly black mask, and was waving a wand around.

"It means," Karen continued, "that —"

KA-BLAM!

An enormous clap of thunder sounded. Everybody jumped — even Kristy.

"It means," Karen tried again, "that the headless ghost was going to come to Ben Brewer . . . and turn him into a crazy man."

"Ew," said Kristy.

"Ben Brewer was doing everything he could think of to keep the ghost away. He had locked the door and the windows, and he wasn't going to leave the room. Not for anything. Not if he had to go to the bathroom. He'd even put garlic all around the room."

"I thought garlic was to keep vampires away," said Kristy.

"Ben wasn't taking any chances," David Michael informed her.

"So imagine this," said Karen. "It's almost midnight, and Ben is locked up in that room. It's all quiet —"

"Except for the storm," said Andrew.

"And the fire crackling," added David Michael.

"And just think," said Karen. "This was happening right here in *our* house . . . in that room on the third floor." (Ben Brewer is Andrew and Karen's great-grandfather.)

"The room we never go in," whispered Andrew.

At that moment, Boo-Boo, the Brewers' fat cat, waddled in.

Karen pointed to him. "Boo-Boo knows about that room, Kristy. He knows it's haunted."

"The whole third floor is," said David Michael. He shuddered. "Boo-Boo doesn't go up to the third floor — *ever.*"

Boo-Boo plopped down next to Karen. He sat on the floor with his tail twitching.

"Relax, Boo-Boo," said Kristy.

"He can't," Karen said. "Do you know where we're sitting? We're right under Ben Brewer's room."

"Aughh!" cried David Michael.

"Karen," said Kristy, "the last time you told ghost stories, you said Boo-Boo won't go on the third floor because it's under the attic and the *attic* is haunted."

Karen paused. "Oh," she said. "Well, that's true. But Ben's room is haunted, too. So anyway," she went on. "It was almost midnight. Just eleven more seconds." She paused. "Eleven . . . ten . . . nine . . . eight . . . seven . . . six . . . five . . . four . . . three . . . two . . ."

(Kristy noticed that she and the boys were all leaning anxiously toward Karen.)

"*One,*" said Karen.

"What happened then?" whimpered Andrew. He sounded near tears. Kristy pulled him into her lap.

"Ben thought there was no way to get in the room. But he was wrong. The ghost came down the *chimney.*"

Everyone turned slightly and eyed the fireplace in the playroom.

"The ghost began to speak," Karen went on. "'Oooh,' it wailed. 'I've come for you, Ben Brewer.'"

At that, Boo-Boo leaped straight into the air, darted through the door, and slid out into the hall, claws flying. Louie awoke, startled, heard Boo-Boo in the hall, and took off after him.

"It's Ben Brewer!" screamed Karen. "It's his crazy ghost! He was haunted — and now he's haunting us!"

"Karen, calm down," said Kristy, whose teeth were chattering. "There is no ghost here."

"Yes, there is! That's why Boo-Boo and Louie are scared! Animals can tell when ghosts are around!"

Andrew burst into tears. "I don't want a ghost here!" he sobbed.

"There's *no ghost,*" said Kristy. She stood up. "Anyway, it's bedtime."

"I want to sleep with you tonight!" wailed Andrew.

"Me, too!" cried Karen.

"Me, too!" cried David Michael.

Kristy admitted (but only to herself and later to the rest of us baby-sitters) that she was glad they wanted to sleep with her. And since she has this mammoth new bed in her room at Watson's, she figured they'd all fit. She hadn't counted on Boo-Boo and Louie joining them, but they did.

Kristy woke up the next morning when she heard whispering and snickering at her door. She blinked her eyes and struggled to sit up. Outside, the sun was shining. Next to her, Karen was sprawled on her back, her mouth open, and one arm slung across Andrew, who was sucking his thumb. On her other side, David Michael was snoring lightly. Louie and Boo-Boo were scrunched up at the end of the bed.

"Look at that!" whispered a voice.

Sam and Charlie were peering into Kristy's room, trying to control their laughter.

"Hey, Kristy, what were you guys *do*ing last night?" exclaimed Sam. "You weren't by any chance afraid of the storm, were you?"

"No," replied Kristy. "Not exactly." She crawled over her brother and slid off the bed.

"You were, too," said Sam. "What a bunch of chickens."

"We were not," Kristy repeated more fiercely. "We were just . . ."

"Just what?" asked Charlie.

"Trust me," said Kristy. "It's a *long* story."

CHAPTER 8

Okay, so Kristy had a bad night. Maybe it was because of my ghost stories, maybe not. But she wasn't the only one having trouble during the storm. Jeff and I had a little trouble of our own . . . an adventure. And we weren't any braver about it than Kristy was with her adventure.

I did a strange thing after I found the secret passage. I didn't tell anyone about it. I'd been so excited — thinking I was like Nancy Drew and all — and then I was so scared when I realized the passageway had a ghost, that by the time I had climbed back into the barn and closed the trapdoor, I was totally confused. So I didn't call any of my friends to tell them the news, and I didn't show the passage to Jeff or my mom. I kept the secret to myself.

But on the night of the second big storm — the night Kristy was baby-sitting for Andrew, Karen, and David Michael — I was sitting for Jeff, and the haunted passage was weighing on my mind.

My mother left at seven o'clock that evening to go out on a date with this man named Mr. Gwynne, which put me in a bad mood. I don't mind if Mom dates, as long as she dates Mary Anne's father. Mary Anne and I want to be step-sisters. But Mom had been going out with several different men. One of them was the son of friends of my grandparents, two were from her office, and a couple more were men she'd met at some party. I didn't like any of them, and I didn't want any of them for a stepfather. (I only wanted Mr. Spier, because of Mary Anne.) Jeff didn't like any of the new men, either.

Tonight, Mom was going out with the son of my grandparents' friends. They were going to have dinner in a restaurant, then go to Granny and Pop-Pop's for dessert. I didn't like the sound of that — much too serious.

So I wasn't in a very good mood as my mom was rushing out the door. Usually I check her over to make sure nothing is mismatched or out of place. But that evening, I sulked in the living room and didn't look at her. If I'd looked at her and seen something wrong, I'd have to have told her. I couldn't let her go out wearing one hoop earring and one pearl earring, or just one false eyelash or something. But I figured that what I didn't know wouldn't hurt me — or her (much).

"I'm leaving, kids!" Mom called from the front door.

"Bye," I said. I was sitting in an armchair, facing away from her. I didn't turn around.

"If it rains, close the windows."

" 'Kay."

"Dawn? Everything all right, honey?"

"Yup."

Mom hesitated. I couldn't see her, but I could *feel* that she was hesitating.

Jeff came crashing down the stairs, taking about three steps at a time.

"Bye, Mom," he said.

"Bye, honey. I just told Dawn — close the windows if it rains. Oh, and there's a casserole in the fridge. Remember, Dawn's in charge."

"Good-bye, Mom," I said pointedly.

Mom took the hint and left, and then I felt really bad.

Jeff didn't notice. "Let's eat," he said.

"All right." Maybe it would take my mind off Mom and the ghost.

Jeff and I heated up the casserole and made a salad. We ate our supper in front of the TV, watching a rerun of *All in the Family.*

"I hate this show," I commented.

"Me, too," Jeff replied.

"Why are we watching it?"

"I don't know. Because it's —"

CRASH!

Thunder. Then rain poured down without warning.

"Windows!" I cried. We abandoned our meal and ran around, closing windows.

Then we tried to eat again, but we had no sooner settled down in front of the TV than the electricity went off. Since it was almost dark outside, it was pitch black inside.

"Yipes!" cried Jeff.

"I wonder if it's off everywhere or just in our neighborhood," I said. *Or maybe,* I thought, *it's just us.* I shivered.

We stood at the front door and looked up and down our street. No lights anywhere, so the power was off in the neighborhood, at least.

Maybe my mother would have to come home. Maybe the rest of her date would be off, along with the electricity. The thought cheered me.

"We better turn off the TV set so it won't come

blaring on when the power's restored," I said. "And let's try to rinse off our dishes. Otherwise, they'll be impossible to clean later."

Jeff groped around and found a flashlight. We cleaned up the kitchen as best we could. Then we wandered through the house.

"Well, this is boring," said Jeff.

"Yeah," I agreed.

"What can you do in the dark?"

I thought for a moment. I hadn't returned *Ghosts and Spooks, Chills and Thrills* to the library yet. I had two more stories to go. And there were a few I wanted to reread. I thought of the ghost in our secret passage and began to feel scared — not the awful kind of scared I'd felt several times earlier in the week — but deliciously scared.

"Hey, Jeff. Want to hear some really great stories?" I asked.

Jeff looked skeptical. (At least by the light of the flashlight, he looked skeptical.) "What kind of stories?" he asked.

"Ghost stories," I whispered.

"Aw . . ."

"I know you don't believe in ghosts, but try to get in the *spirit* of things," I told him. "Get it? Spirit? Look. It's a gloomy, rainy, spooky night. Besides, what else is there to do?"

"Nothing," replied Jeff.

"Okay. Come on up to my room."

Ghosts and Spooks was waiting for us on my nightstand. We sat on my bed and I took the flashlight from Jeff and opened the book. First I read him "Things Unseen." Then I read him the story about the phantom hitchhiker. Then I read him "The Haunting of Weatherstaff Moor."

Before I got to one of the new ones at the end of the book, Jeff turned to me and said, "Let's stop now, Dawn."

"Had enough?" I asked.

He nodded. I couldn't tell if he was bored, scared, or sleepy.

"*Now* what should we do?" he asked. From the way he sounded, I decided he was bored.

"Let's try to play a game by flashlight," I suggested.

We tried. It was next to impossible. There was never enough light, even after Jeff perched the flashlight in a sort of sling made from a dish towel that he suspended from the edge of a table.

"I give up," I said.

Jeff yawned hugely. "What a waste of a Friday night," he said. "Do you know all the great TV shows we're missing?"

"Wellll," I said slowly. "There *is* something we could do, and all we need is a flashlight."

"What?" Jeff looked mildly interested.

"Back to my room," I ordered.

I led Jeff up the stairs again and straight to the wall with the fancy molding.

"Watch this," I said. "Here, hold the light."

I pressed a corner of the molding (it hadn't taken long to figure out how the catch worked), and the wall swung inward.

Jeff gasped. "Hey! Hey, what . . . ?"

"I discovered this a couple of days ago," I told him. "It's a real, honest-to-goodness secret passage."

"I don't believe it," said Jeff flatly.

"Come on. Want to see it?"

I'd taken the button and buckle and key out of the passage and hidden them in one of my bureau drawers. Somehow, without the *evidence* of the ghost, the ghost himself seemed less scary.

"Come on," I said again. I grabbed Jeff's hand and pulled him into the passage. "I didn't say anything because I — I just wanted a secret, I guess. But anyway, isn't this great?"

Wide-eyed, Jeff followed me through the passage to the rickety old steps. He had to walk behind me. The passage wasn't wide enough for two.

We were just about to start down the stairs when Jeff said, "Stop, Dawn. Look at that!"

"What?" I cried.

"Let me have the flashlight for a sec."

I handed it to him and he shined it against the wall near the top step. I could see something gleaming there. An image of the things I'd squirreled away in my bureau came to mind.

Jeff brushed aside a dust bunny with his foot. Then he stooped down and picked up the object.

"What is it?" I asked. I tried to sound calm, but if my heart was beating as loudly as I thought it was, my brother could probably hear it, too.

Jeff examined the object in the light.

"It's a nickel," he said, sounding puzzled. "At least, it says 'five cents' on it, but it doesn't look like any nickel I've ever seen. There's a picture of a Native American man on one side and a buffalo on the other. Maybe it's foreign. . . . No, it's from the U.S."

"Buffalo nickels are *real* old," I informed him. "They made those nickels before the ones they make now. Let's see the date on that."

Jeff and I turned the nickel over and over and

around and around, but it was rubbed so smooth we couldn't find a date.

"It must have worn off," said Jeff.

"Gosh, if it's worn off, this nickel must be ancient. It takes forever for metal to wear down."

"Yeah," agreed Jeff. "I wonder how it got here."

"Good question," I muttered, but Jeff didn't hear me.

"Well, let's go," he said.

Jeff was in front now and he led the way down the stairs. We had rounded the corner and were heading through the long tunnel to the barn when something crunched under my foot. I let out a cry. I was sure it was bones . . . part of a skeleton.

"What was that?" cried Jeff.

"Oh, I don't want to know," I moaned.

Jeff played the flashlight beam around on the floor. A few inches from my left foot, it lit up a small brown mound. Jeff and I bent down.

"I think it's part of an ice-cream cone," I said, although Jeff and I have eaten maybe two cones in our health-food lives.

"Really?" Jeff replied. "I thought ice-cream cones were kind of yellow and, you know, airy looking. And they have flat bottoms. Don't they? Remember that time Dad took us to Dairy Queen?

What's left of that thing," he went on, touching the mound with the toe of his sneaker, "is brown and hard and has a pointed bottom."

"You know, I think this is an old-fashioned ice-cream cone," I said. I felt scared, awed, and excited at the same time. I wondered how long the cone had been in the passage. More important, I wondered why I hadn't seen either the cone or the nickel the other day. Can ghosts make things materialize? I was *sure* they hadn't been there before.

"Um, Jeff," I managed to say, "I don't want to scare you, but this passage is haunted — by an angry ghost. The ghost of someone who was locked up here to die a long time ago."

"Oh, for cripe's sakes," said Jeff. He gave me a really disgusted look. "You have got to be kidding."

"No, I'm not," I replied in a hushed voice.

"Okay," said Jeff, "the passage is haunted. . . . Prove it."

"I don't think I can *prove* it," I told him, "but I have been hearing an awful lot of weird noises lately. Mom keeps saying things like 'the house is settling.'"

"She's right," said Jeff.

"Houses *moan* when they settle?"

Jeff looked startled. "Moan?"

"Yeah. Like this." I tried to imitate the moaning I'd heard.

"It could have been the storm," Jeff said, but he didn't look convinced, especially when I added disdainfully, "I *do* know the difference between something howling outside and something moaning inside."

"Well . . ."

"And," I went on, "the cone and the nickel weren't here the day I discovered the passage. I went looking pretty carefully, and I found a buckle and a button and a key. But these things weren't here."

"What are you saying?" asked Jeff, looking nervous in the flickering light.

"I'm saying that until right now, I didn't tell *anyone* about the passage. So no one's been in it except me, right?"

"Right."

"So where did the cone and the nickel come from?"

Jeff didn't answer. His eyes were growing wide, and he couldn't seem to close his mouth.

"There's only one answer," I told him. "A ghost. And I'll tell you something else. I don't think I should have taken those other things out of the passage. I think the ghost is mad and wants them back. And we better not take these, either. Go put the nickel back where you found it."

"*Me?* I'm not putting it back. Not alone, anyway." Jeff now looked truly terrified. His voice had risen to a squeak.

"Well, I'm not coming with you. We're much closer to the other end of the passage. I want to get out of here."

Jeff scowled at me. "Look at it this way," he said. "I've got the flashlight. If I go, the light goes with me. You'll be left alone in the dark."

I paused. He had a point. "Okay," I said. "Anyway, I just realized that we might as well both turn around now. We have to take the passage back to my room after all. It's pouring outside."

"Where *is* the other end of the passage?" asked Jeff.

"In the barn."

And at that moment we heard a creak, followed by a moan.

"Aughhh!" we yelled. Without another word of discussion, we turned and ran headlong through the passage, up the stairs, and back to my room. Jeff dropped the nickel somewhere as we ran.

CHAPTER 9

Somehow Jeff and I had managed to forget about the power failure. We had burst out of the passage and into my room, and I had slammed the wall shut behind us before we realized we were still in total darkness. It wasn't very comforting.

We flopped down on my bed, breathing heavily.

"It was the ghost!" I cried. "And he's carrying a grudge that's probably a hundred years old."

Cre-e-e-ak. Cre-e-e-ak.

Jeff and I jumped a mile. "I think the ghost's in the passage right *now*!" Jeff cried.

I'm sure I turned pale. I felt my knees go weak. "I'm calling Mom!" I announced, wondering if I could stand up without collapsing.

"Oh, good," said Jeff. He grabbed me at the waist, and followed me out of my room and into Mom's. We looked like two little kids playing choo-choo train.

As I reached for the phone, Jeff said helpfully, "I hope the telephone is still working."

I drew my hand back. "What if it isn't?" I whispered.

For a moment, neither of us spoke. At last, I reached my hand out again. I picked up the receiver and brought it to my ear very slowly. Halfway there, I could hear the dial tone. "Oh, thank you, thank you, *thank* you," I said to no one in particular.

I figured Mom and her date would be at Granny and Pop-Pop's by then, so I called their house. Pop-Pop answered the phone, and I got carried away and told him we were having an emergency.

When Mom got to the phone, she sounded breathless and nervous. "Honey? Are you and Jeff all right?" she asked.

"Mom!" I exclaimed. "The power's off here, it's all dark, and there's this secret passage from my room to the barn — I know I should have told you about it, but I didn't — and Jeff and I looked in it, and we have a ghost."

"We heard noises!" Jeff shouted into the receiver from behind me.

"Dawn. Slow down. What are you saying?" asked my mother.

"I found a secret passage in our house. A real one." I paused. "Mom, the power's off here. Jeff and I are in the dark, except for a flashlight."

"I understand that, honey. But we've had power failures before. Now what is this about a secret passage?"

"You know how I'm always looking for one?" I asked.

"Yes."

"Well, I found one the other day. I promise it's not a figment of my imagination or anything. But I kept it a secret. I didn't even tell Mary Anne."

"And where is this passage?"

"It runs from under the barn — there's a trap-door in the floor — to my room. You know the wall with all the molding? It swings out into my room when you press a corner of the molding."

"Are you positive, Dawn?"

"*Yes*. Cross my heart and hope to die. And tonight Jeff got bored, so I decided to show him the passage. We'd almost gotten to the other end when we heard these noises. It really did sound like —"

Mom interrupted me before I could finish.

"Trip and I will be right there. Sit tight, stay calm, and *don't* go back in the passage." She hung up.

"So?" Jeff said as soon as I'd hung up the phone, too. We both felt a little more relaxed. "What'd she say?"

"Mr. Gwynne's name is Trip," was all I could answer. "*Trip*. Can you believe it?"

Jeff laughed. "Oh, yeah. Man, that is *so cool*," he said sarcastically.

"I bet he wears pink socks and alligator shirts and his friends call him, like, the Trip-Man or something."

"I bet he plays golf," said Jeff, with a snort of laughter.

"I bet his idea of an amusing afternoon is balancing his checkbook. And," I added, "I bet he has real short hair, wears wire-rim glasses, and has gray eyes, but wears contacts to make them look blue."

Jeff laughed so hard that he collapsed on the floor. I joined him — but mid-collapse I let out a yelp.

"What is it?" cried Jeff.

"What are we laughing for? That ghost could be sneaking into my room this very second. We've got to go block the wall off!"

"In the *dark*?"

"Do you want the ghost in here with us?"

"No." Jeff flew out of Mom's room and into mine before I'd even gotten up off the floor. "Shove something in front of the wall," he commanded as soon as I ran in.

We moved my dresser in front of the door to the passage. Then we put a chair on top of it, and, puffing hard, slid my bed against the front of the dresser.

We were unloading books from my shelves and piling them on the chair and bed when two things happened at once: the power was restored, and Mom and Mr. Gwynne came home. When the lights flicked on, Mom found Jeff and me standing on my bed, stacking books onto a pile of furniture. And Jeff and I saw two people standing in a doorway that we thought was empty.

Everyone screamed.

"What are you doing?" cried Mom at the same time that I yelled, "When did you get here?"

Then we answered each other at the same time, too. "Keeping the ghost out," I replied as Mom said, "Just now."

"Whoa! Everybody calm down," exclaimed Mom's date.

Jeff and I jumped to the floor.

"Kids," said my mother, who was trying to catch her breath. "This is Mr. Gwynne. Theodore Gwynne."

(My mother had no idea why Jeff and I looked at each other and began to laugh then.)

"And," she went on, ignoring us, "this is Dawn, and this is Jeff."

"Hi," the three of us said uncomfortably.

I have to admit that the Trip-Man didn't look exactly as Jeff and I had imagined, but he was pretty close. He was wearing glasses, but not wire-rims. The frames were tortoise-shell and very round. His blond hair was short, but behind the glasses, his eyes were brown. He was wearing a suit and tie, so there were no alligators anywhere, and his socks weren't pink but his shirt was.

"Dawn," said Mom, sounding exasperated, "what are you and Jeff *do*ing?"

"Blocking the entrance to the secret passage so no one can come in."

"You mean the ghost?" she asked with a smile.

"Yeah."

"I thought ghosts could float right through walls."

"Um . . ." I said. (Why hadn't *I* thought of that?) "Of course they can. But the passage is his home base." What a stupid excuse.

And now I had something new to worry about.

"Well, let's just see what we have here," said the Trip-Man.

He and Jeff and I moved the books and furniture away from the wall. Then I pressed the molding and the wall opened up.

Mom gasped. I don't think she'd really believed I'd found a secret passage until then.

The Trip-Man held out his hand. "If you'll let me have the flashlight, I'll go take a look-see," he said.

A look-see?

Jeff handed him the flashlight.

"Oh, Trip, do you think you should?" asked Mom.

(Jeff and I dissolved into giggles again.)

My mother peered through the opening into the dark tunnel. She watched the Trip-Man disappear. "*How* did you discover this, Dawn?" I told her the whole story, explaining where the passage led.

"I just can't believe it," said Mom. "I know this is an old house, but . . ." Her voice trailed off.

When the Trip-Man returned, he looked dusty but was in one piece. "There's no one — and *nothing* —" he added, looking at me, "in the passage. If you heard noises, I'm sure they were just —"

"The storm," I supplied. "Or the house settling."

The Trip-Man cleared his throat. "Right," he said. "By the way, I found this." He opened one hand and extended the ghost's Buffalo nickel toward me.

I just barely managed not to scream as I took it.

"I suggest," the Trip-Man went on, talking to Mom, "that tomorrow morning you figure out some way to lock both entrances to the passage, or at least the entrance in the barn. I'm sure no one knows about the passage, but since it *is* another way into your home, you should lock it as you would any door."

"Definitely," agreed Mom.

"Well, that'll keep *people* out," I said, "but what about the ghost?"

"Dawn," Mom began warningly.

"There *is* one," I said. "The ghost of the secret passage." I explained how I knew that the passage was haunted.

My mother and the Trip-Man began to look incredibly impatient. They didn't even let me tell them about the ice-cream cone and the meaning of the nickel. Mom waved me to a stop.

A few minutes later, the Trip-Man left. Mom walked him out to his car.

Jeff reluctantly went to bed.

I looked around my room. No way was I going to sleep in there. I gathered up a blanket, a pillow, and *Thrills and Chills*. Before I took everything down to the living room, though, I opened the molded wall a crack and tossed the Buffalo nickel back to the ghost in the passageway.

Mom went upstairs to her bedroom. I thought she was crazy. After all, the secret passage ran between our rooms. Mom was as close to the ghost as I was.

I was just settling down on the couch when I saw Mom's purse on the floor in the dining room. She is *so* scatterbrained. *I really should take it upstairs to her*, I thought, heaving myself off the couch. But when I picked up the purse, I saw that it had been sitting on something, a tattered old book called *A History of Stoneybrooke*. It must have come from Granny. She never sends any of us home empty-handed. Sometimes she gives us food, but mostly little treasures and keepsakes. Mom says it's Granny's way of making sure she gives the things she loves best to the people she loves best before she dies. (As if she's going to die any time soon. She's only about sixty or sixty-three or something.)

The book I was holding was so old it was falling apart. The title was written in gold, but the gold had mostly rubbed off. The binding was peeling away, and two of the corners of the cover had cracked off. Gingerly, I opened the book to the first page. *A History of Stoneybrooke*, it said again. By Enos Cotterling. Copyright MDCCCLXXII. I dredged up an old arithmetic lesson (where was Stacey's math brain when I needed it?), and decided the book had been published in 1872. Over a hundred years ago! Stoneybrooke . . . was that our town — Stoneybrook? When had the *e* been dropped? A line of teeny-tiny print said that the book had been published by Tynedale Press, right here in town.

I forgot all about Mom's purse and wandered back to the couch, turning pages as I went. The table of contents looked pretty boring — taxation, imports and exports, trade, growth of town, property laws. But the very last chapter sounded interesting. It was called, simply, *Legends*.

I turned carefully to the back of the book. Two pages fell out, and I replaced them guiltily, even though I knew I hadn't done anything wrong.

"Like most New England towns," the chapter began, "Stoneybrooke is replete with Native American myths and legends. But one local legend, not to be discounted lightly, is the unsolved mystery of Mister Jared Mullray." That did it. I was hooked. I started reading in earnest.

It seemed that long before Enos Cotterling had written his history, around the year 1810, a family in Stoneybrooke, the Mullrays, had fallen into financial trouble. They were deeply in debt to a banker named Mathias Bradford and couldn't pay their bills. The only things they owned that were worth much at all were their home, "a clapboard structure out past the Smythe property," and their small farm, Wood Acres. In order to pay off their debts, the Mullrays were forced to sell both, including their furniture and many of their belongings.

Old Man Mullray wanted to move up to Peacham, a tiny, young town in Vermont, and he convinced his wife, his daughter, his son-in-law, and their three children to move with him. There, he said, they could start over. But he could not convince his younger son, thirty-year-old Jared, to go with them. Jared, the author wrote, had never been "quite right in the head." He loved Wood Acres — a little too much.

Early on a Monday morning, the Mullrays packed a few personal belongings onto a cart, saddled up one of their horses, and prepared to leave. Mathias Bradford, who was going to sell off the farm, arrived with some men from the bank just as the Mullrays were tossing their last bag onto the cart.

"Jared!" shouted Old Man Mullray.

"I ain't leaving!" was the reply everyone heard. But Mr. Bradford was to say later that it didn't sound as if his voice was coming from the house *or* the barn — sort of somewhere in between, although no one could *see* him anywhere.

(A clap of thunder sounded, and I shivered, pulling my blanket more tightly around me.)

Old Man Mullray glanced at this wife, who shrugged sadly. Then he flicked the reins, and the horse plodded down the lane. The Mullrays left Wood Acres behind forever.

Now, Mathias Bradford and four other men (one of whom was the head of the town council) had watched the Mullrays drive off without Jared. And they had heard his disembodied voice say that he wasn't leaving. But although the house and barn were searched thoroughly as every last stick of furniture and every last harness were sold off, no one ever saw Jared again. He simply disappeared.

A few people said he had packed up and moved to Alaska, but Mr. Bradford didn't believe that. He had heard Jared and was convinced he'd never leave. The only question was — where *was* he? Soon another rumor began to circulate about Jared, and the people of Stoneybrooke were more inclined to believe this one. They thought that Jared, who couldn't bear to leave Wood Acres, was still there . . . somewhere. They thought he must know about some secret hiding place, and that he stayed there by day and scavenged for food at night.

Decades passed. By the time Enos Cotterling was writing his history, he presumed that Jared was dead. In fact, the story about Jared had become a ghost story. Jared, people said, had died in his secret hiding place, but his spirit remained. Wood Acres (which had been swallowed up by another, larger, farm and was no longer called Wood Acres) was haunted by Jared, who was always on the prowl not only for food, but for trinkets and things that he could sell in order to try to pay back Mr. Bradford.

I put the book down thoughtfully. Wood

Acres, a ghost, a secret hiding pl . . . A secret hiding place! Suddenly, my arms broke out in crawly gooseflesh. I shivered so hard my teeth chattered.

It fit! Everything fit! Enos Cotterling hadn't described where Wood Acres was, but it must be my house and my barn! The house was old enough, it had once been part of a farm, and there certainly was a good hiding place on the property . . . a place you could yell from and sound as if you were between the house and the barn, yet not be seen.

There really was a ghost in our secret passage, and that ghost was crazy Jared Mullray!

CHAPTER 10

Sunday

There are times when I think
babysitting is the hardest thing in th
world. Last nigt was one those times.
I was baby siting for Jamie Newton.
And Lucy. Lucy was an angle, but Jamie
wasn't. Boy! I have never seen him
like that. All I was trying to do was
put him to bed. That's all. I didn't
have to give him diner or anything.
I just had to get him to sleep. And
I really wanted to too. Because there
was this good program on tv I wanted
to see it but Jamie WOULD NOT GO TO
SLEEP!

It was eight o'clock when Claudia reached the Newtons'. Her job that night really should have been one of the easiest in baby-sitting history. Lucy was already in her crib and sound asleep. Jamie had already eaten dinner. Mr. and Mrs. Newton were only going to be gone for two hours. All Claudia had to do was put Jamie to bed — and the evening was hers.

That's how the evening *should* have gone. There was just one problem: Jamie didn't want to go to bed. I mean, he *really* didn't want to go to bed.

When Claudia rang the Newtons' doorbell that night, Jamie answered it. Right away, Claudia could tell he was wound up.

"Hi-hi! Hi-hi! Hi-hi!" he greeted her.

"Hi-hi, Jamie," said Claud.

Jamie was jumping up and down, up and down, like a yo-yo in blue jeans. "I learned a new song!" he exclaimed. "Listen to this: I'm in love with a big blue frog. A big blue frog loves me. It's not as bad as it may seem. He wears glasses and he's six foot three. Oh —"

Jamie's song was interrupted by his father. Mr. Newton rolled his eyes. "I'm sorry I taught him that," he said. "He's been singing it *all day*. And there are several more verses."

Claudia laughed. "I think it's funny," she said.

"Only the first seventy-five times," replied Mr. Newton, but he was smiling.

Mrs. Newton came down the stairs as Claudia stepped inside. "'Hi, honey," she said. "Well, the baby's asleep, and Jamie has eaten. I don't think he needs a bath tonight —"

"Yea!" interrupted Jamie.

"So just put his pj's on him. He's had a long day and should go to bed —" (she glanced at Jamie, who was listening intently) "— s-o-o-n," she spelled out.

"No fair spelling, Mommy!" Jamie protested.

"Okay," Claudia said to Mrs. Newton. Then she added, "Don't worry, Jamie. We'll have fun tonight before you go to bed."

"Goody."

The Newtons left then, and Jamie began hopping up and down again.

"Okay, Jamie. Time to put your pj's on," said Claudia.

"Already?" he whined.

"Yup. It's almost bedtime. Come on upstairs."

"Just let me show you this one thing first. . . . Okay?"

"Okay," Claudia relented. "Just *one* thing."

"It's down in the playroom." Jamie took Claudia by the hand and led her down a flight of stairs to the Newtons' rec room. He stood in the middle of the room and looked around.

"What is it?" asked Claudia.

"It's, um . . ." Jamie put his finger in his mouth. "It's this!" He darted over to a beat-up dump truck. "Look at it," he said.

"Your old truck?" asked Claudia, puzzled.

Jamie paused. "Oh, no. That wasn't it. I meant . . ." He picked up a little wooden cow that was lying next to the truck. "I meant my cow."

"Jamie," said Claudia, growing suspicious.

"No, I meant my — my Beary Bear," he said, snatching up a stuffed animal.

"That was three things, Jame-o," Claudia pointed out gently. "Time to go upstairs now."

"Can I wear my Paddington Bear pajamas, Claudy?" asked Jamie.

"Sure," replied Claudia, glad he was actually thinking about bed.

"Good," said Jamie, "'Cause they're in the wash."

"Then I'm afraid you can't wear them." Claudia led Jamie back upstairs.

"But you just said I could."

"I didn't know they were in the wash when I said that. You can't wear them if they're dirty."

"Let's wash them," suggested Jamie.

"Sorry. That'll take too much time. We'd have to dry them, too."

"How long would it take?"

"Too long."

"How many minutes?"

"Twelve hundred and forty-nine," replied Claudia.

"Wow," said Jamie.

Claudia and Jamie tiptoed past Lucy's room and into Jamie's. Claudia pointed to his bed. "Look," she said. "Mommy laid out your farm pajamas."

Jamie made a face. "I don't want to wear them. They're for babies. They have baby stuff all over them."

Claudia looked at them. They *were* sort of babyish. "Let's choose a different pair, then." She opened his bureau and brought out two more pairs. "Which ones?" she asked. (She was careful not to say, "Do you want to wear either of these?" Jamie might have said "No.")

Jamie pointed to one pair.

"Great," said Claud. "Okay, off with your shirt." She waited for Jamie to raise his arms so she could slip his shirt off.

"I'll do it myself," said Jamie. "You leave."

"Leave!" exclaimed Claudia. Jamie was too

young to be getting modest. "How about if I turn my back?"

Jamie considered the offer. "Okay," he said at last. "But don't peek."

Claudia sat cross-legged on Jamie's bed, facing the wall. The room grew very quiet. Claudia studied the pattern of the wallpaper. "Jamie?" she asked after a minute or two had gone by.

No answer.

"Is it all right if I turn around to see how you're doing?"

Silence.

Very slowly, Claudia swiveled around. Jamie was gone.

"Jamie!" Claudia cried as loudly as she dared. (She didn't want to wake Lucy.)

Claudia ran through the hallway, pausing to peek into the bathroom. No Jamie. She ran down the stairs and into the kitchen. No Jamie. She ran down the last flight of steps and into the playroom.

"Hi-hi!" said Jamie brightly, but he looked a bit sheepish. He was riding a toy car and was still fully dressed.

"James Anderson Newton. You were supposed to put your pj's on," said Claudia. "I'm beginning to lose my patience. Now go back to

98

your room, please. And this time I'm not going to turn my back."

Jamie scowled, but he did as Claudia said. When he was finally in his pajamas, Claudia tucked him in bed.

"Oops," he said. "I forgot to brush my teeth. And I ate cookies after dinner. Cookies have sugar, and sugar makes calories in your teeth."

Claudia had to smile. "Cavities," she told him. "All right. Into the bathroom."

Jamie scampered down the hall. (Claudia had the sense to follow him.) Standing at the sink, he squeezed about a yard of toothpaste onto his brush and worked it around in his mouth, creating a great amount of foam. He rinsed and spat six times. Claudia waited patiently.

When he was done, he dashed down the hall and leaped into his bed.

"How about a story?" asked Claudia.

"Oops," said Jamie. "I forgot to go to the bathroom." He ran down the hall again, and returned a few minutes later.

"*Now*," said Claudia. "How about a story?"

"Oops," said Jamie. "I forgot to get a drink of water."

"I'll get it," said Claudia. "You stay right here. Don't move a muscle."

Claudia filled a paper cup with water and brought it to Jamie. He was sitting in exactly the same position as he'd been in when she'd left the room. She handed the cup to him.

Jamie didn't reach for it.

"Here you go," said Claudia.

"An I oove?" asked Jamie, barely moving his lips.

"What?"

"An I oove?"

"Can you move?"

"Yeh."

"Of course you can move."

"But you said 'don't move a muscle.'"

"Claudia sighed. "I just meant don't go anywhere. And you didn't. Here. Drink your water."

Jamie took the cup and drank.

"All right," said Claudia. She pulled a book off his shelf. "Let's read *Harold and the Purple Crayon*."

Claudia read the story to Jamie. When she was finished he said, "Now can we read *Make Way for Ducklings*?"

"Oh, Jame-o," said Claud. "I'm sorry, but that one's too long."

"Please, please, please? Pretty puh-*lease* with a cherry on top?"

Against her better judgment, Claudia gave in. It took nearly a half an hour to read the story because Jamie kept interrupting her to ask questions.

"But," he said, as Claudia was closing the book, "why did Mr. Mallard leave Mrs. Mallard and the ducklings all alone?"

"He was waiting for them at their new home."

"Oh. How come Michael called all the policemen?"

"Because," replied Claud, "the duck family needed help. Now into bed."

Jamie crawled under the covers. He asked for another drink of water . . . and another. Finally, he seemed sleepy.

Claudia tiptoed downstairs and settled herself in front of the TV. She'd been watching for about five minutes when she heard a voice behind her say, "But how come Mr. Mallard just waited on the island? And can I have another drink of water?"

CHAPTER 11

"You know what I think?" asked Mary Anne dreamily.

"What?" I replied.

The two of us were lying on our backs in the hayloft in the barn. The day was stickily warm and sunny, and I could see particles of dust floating through the sunshine that streamed through the cracks in the walls. It was only the third time Mary Anne had ever been in the barn. She's such a 'fraidy cat. Just because the barn is a little rickety.

As if reading my thoughts, she went on, "I think I'm too afraid of things."

I couldn't disagree with her.

"And being afraid always makes things worse than they really are. I was afraid of boys before Stacey and I went to Sea City. I was afraid of making new friends before I met you."

"You were afraid of the barn," I pointed out.

"Yup," Mary Anne glanced through the copy of *Sixteen* magazine that was lying between us.

"Are you feeling braver now?" I asked her.

"Sure," she said absentmindedly. "Gosh, look at this kid Cam Geary. Isn't he adorable?"

"Yeah . . . How brave are you feeling?"

"Pretty brave. I wish Cam lived here in Stoneybrook."

"How'd you like to prove to me just how brave you've become?"

"Huh?" Mary Anne finally dragged her eyeballs away from Cam Geary.

"I said, 'How'd you like to prove how brave you've become?'"

"What do you mean?" asked Mary Anne suspiciously.

"I've got a great secret to show you."

"You do?"

"Yes. But you're going to have to be very, very brave. Come on!" I jumped up. "Come in the house with me and we'll get flashlights."

"Flashlights?" repeated Mary Anne. "Whatever this is — I guess it has to do with the dark?"

"Right. But you're not afraid of the dark, are you?"

"No. I'm afraid of all the things I can't see that the dark is hiding."

"Oh, Mary *Anne*. I thought you said you were getting so brave."

"Yeah, well . . ."

I couldn't admit that I wasn't feeling particularly brave myself. What I wanted to do, of course, was show Mary Anne the secret passage. I hadn't had the nerve to go in it, let alone talk about it, since the night I'd read about Jared Mullray. I wanted someone to come with me. I also wanted someone to be able to share the amazing secret.

I got to my feet and picked up the magazine. "Let's go," I said, trying to sound enthusiastic. "You are in for the surprise of your life."

Mary Anne and I climbed out of the hayloft. We went into our house and found a couple of flashlights. Then I led Mary Anne to my bedroom.

I had decided to enter the passage from the house instead of the barn. For one thing, seeing my wall swing open was a lot more dramatic than shoving in the dusty old trapdoor. For another, it was a lot less scary. And if we left the wall open, it would let some light into the passage.

"Okay. Get ready," I said. I pressed the molding and the wall began to open up. I turned around to watch Mary Anne's reaction.

It was worth it. All she was able to do was let her mouth drop open, cover it with both hands, and stare.

"I found it," I said unnecessarily. "A secret passage."

"Oh, wow. I don't believe it." Mary Anne's voice was little more than a whisper. "How — how did you find it?"

I told her the story, but I left out all the stuff about the buckle and the nickel and Jared Mullray. I'm no fool. If Mary Anne knew those things, she'd probably never get within a mile of my house again.

"Don't you want to see it?" I asked her. I took her by the arm and edged her toward the wall.

We turned our flashlights on and stepped into the passage. I shoved Mary Anne ahead of me. "You go first," I said.

"Are you crazy?"

"Absolutely not. I know if I go first you won't follow. I'll find you lounging around on my bed or something. Now go. I'll be right here."

Trembling, Mary Anne led the way toward the stairs. By the time we reached them, she was fine, but I was in a panic. I didn't say anything, but I hadn't seen the Buffalo nickel. And I knew very well that I'd tossed it back in the passage after the Trip-Man had given it to me. I wasn't sure how hard I'd thrown it, but it couldn't have gone too far. Certainly not down the stairs. Where was it?

Answer: It was missing. Jared had it. He'd wanted it back. He wanted to give it to Mathias Bradford.

I tried to convince myself I was being ridiculous. As we stepped gingerly down the stairs, I swept the beam of my flashlight carefully from side to side, just in case.

No coin.

Mary Anne and I had almost reached the spot where Jeff and I had heard the weird noises the other night, when Mary Anne stopped dead in her tracks.

"*Shh!*" she hissed. "Did you hear that?"

"Hear what?"

"*Shh!*"

We stopped to listen. I didn't hear a sound, but I saw something at my feet. I leaned over for a look. Peanut shells. They were kicked off to the side and were kind of grimy looking, but I *knew* they hadn't been in the passage before.

"Uh-oh. Oh, *no*," I moaned. I couldn't help it.

"What's wrong?" asked Mary Anne suspiciously.

"Those peanut shells weren't here the last time I was in the passage. I'm positive they weren't. Oh, it's Jared!"

"Jared?" repeated Mary Anne.

"The — the ghost."

"What ghost?" said Mary Anne in a quavery voice.

"The ghost of the secret passage." It was too late for secrets. Besides, Mary Anne is my best friend. I *had* to tell her.

Now I know Mary Anne is timid, but I hadn't really expected her to desert me in the darkness. That's just what she did, though. Without another word, she squeezed by me, clattered along the passage, up the steps, and back to my room.

"How do you close this thing?" I could hear her yelling.

I reached the top of the stairs in time to see the patch of light at the end of the passage growing smaller. Mary Anne was shoving the wall in place.

"Don't close it, you dope!" I yelled. "I'm still in here."

"Oh, sorry," said Mary Anne. "I wasn't thinking."

I slipped through the opening and closed off the passageway.

"Now who's the crazy one?" I gasped, flopping onto my bed.

Mary Anne flopped down beside me. "Not me!" she exclaimed. "You! You brought me some place where there's a ghost!" Suddenly, she stopped and looked at me. "Wait a second. A real ghost? Are you sure you haven't just been reading too many of those weird stories?"

"I'm sure," I replied, starting to get my breath back. "I better tell you everything, though. All right, here's the story."

"The whole story?" interrupted Mary Anne.

"Yes, the whole story. Okay. For starters, I'd been hearing a lot of weird sounds. They were coming from the direction of the passage, only I didn't know there was a passage at first. Then I discovered the passage, just like I told you. The first time I was in it — the day I found it — I came across a button, a buckle, and a key. They were all really old. Here, I'll show you." I got the things out of my bureau drawer and laid them on the bed.

Mary Anne sat up. She peered at the objects. But she wouldn't touch them.

"I bet they're more than a hundred years old," I said. "Maybe more than two hundred years old."

"Wow!" whispered Mary Anne.

"And, see," I continued, "what happened is that someone once hid out in the secret passage. His name was Jared Mullray, and he 'wasn't right in the head.'" I showed Mary Anne the last chapter in *A History of Stoneybrooke.* Then I added in a low, spooky voice, "And now that poor old angry ghost haunts the passage and maybe our house, too, scavenging around for food and for anything he thinks might be valuable."

"Oh, Dawn," said Mary Anne. "You don't have any proof." But she didn't sound very sure of herself.

"Well," I admitted, "not really. But Wood Acres could be our house and barn. And the secret passage would be the perfect hiding place. Anyway, listen to this. The second time I went in the passage, I was with Jeff, and he found a Buffalo nickel. You know what that is?"

Mary Anne nodded.

"I know it wasn't there before. And while we were in the passage, we heard all these weird sounds, moaning and stuff."

"You did?"

"Yes. And when we were in again just now, I looked everywhere for the nickel and it *wasn't there.*"

"You didn't take it out of the passage?"

"Well, I did. I mean, someone did, but I threw it back." I told her about the Trip-Man.

"Did you put the locks on like he suggested?" Mary Anne wanted to know.

"Only on the entrance to my room," I said. "And I only lock it at night. We couldn't figure out a way to lock the trapdoor, so we just set a bale of hay on top of it.

"Anyway," I went on, "the peanut shells weren't in the passage before. They just appeared. And no living person has been in this passage except you, Jeff, and me!"

Mary Anne nodded. Then suddenly she stiffened.

"What?" I asked.

We didn't even have to keep quiet to hear it. The next sound was loud enough to wake the dead.

THUMP.

It definitely came from the secret passage.

Mary Anne started to scream, but I clapped my hand over her mouth. I didn't want Jared to hear us.

The thump was followed by another thump, then nothing.

When the passage had been quiet for ten entire minutes, I jumped up. "I'm going back in there!" I exclaimed.

"Not me," said Mary Anne. "See you later." But she must have felt guilty because a moment later she added, "I'll guard the entrance for you."

I took my flashlight, marched into the passage, and kept going. At the bottom of the stairs, I screamed. Lying at my feet was a book. It was called *Great Dog Tales*. It looked about a hundred years old. I had never seen it before in my life. I turned around and ran back to Mary Anne.

CHAPTER 12

Tuesday

The Pikes strike again! Today I baby-sat for Nicky, Vanessa, Claire, and Margo. Since just the four of them were there, Mrs. Pike decided she needed only one sitter. Believe me, I could have used ten or twelve more. Vanessa and Margo did something to Claire I will never, ever be able to forget. To top it off, Nicky disappeared. I didn't worry at first, but when he didn't turn up after almost an hour, I got nervous. I'm sure he breaks that two-block rule, but I can't prove it. Anyway, get a load of what the girls did.

Oh, boy. Am l glad I wasn't sitting at the Pikes' that day. As it was, I got called in to look for Nicky, but Stacey sure had her hands full with the girls, even before she knew Nicky was gone.

It started when the mail arrived. Usually, the mail in our neighborhood is delivered just before lunch, but that day it was late. The mail truck pulled up at the Pikes' at about three o'clock in the afternoon.

"I'll get it!" cried Vanessa. She tore out the door with Claire and Margo at her heels. Nicky was on the sun porch, alone as usual, reading a book.

Stacey took advantage of the quiet to start in on the list of chores Mrs. Pike had left her. (Sometimes, if Mr. and Mrs. Pike are behind with the house-work, us baby-sitters pitch in with the laundry and stuff, and then we earn mother's helpers wages, which are better than plain old baby-sitters wages.)

Stacey got into the rhythm of folding clean clothes and folded two basketsful. Then she moved on to the kitchen, where she unloaded the clean dishes in the dishwasher and loaded up the dirty ones.

The house was quiet. Stacey sighed content-edly. She checked on Nicky. He was still reading on the porch. She thought she remembered hear-ing the girls come in.

"Vanessa?" she called. "Claire? Margo?"

"We're upstairs!" Vanessa shouted back.

"Okay!"

Stacey returned to her chores.

Fifteen minutes later, things were still quiet. Quiet wasn't unusual for Nicky those days, but it was for the girls. Three girls generally make some sort of noise, but Stacey hadn't heard so much as a giggle.

She started up the stairs — and that was when the *thing* came flying down at her. It was little and shrieked and had a head of white foam. When it collided with Stacey, it left foam all over her Hawaiian shirt.

"Yikes!" cried Stacey. She backed against the wall.

The foam-thing was rubbing at its eyes. It stumbled forward and Stacey caught it before it fell down the stairs.

"Claire!" Stacey exclaimed. "Is that you?"

"Yes," wailed the foam-thing. "It's (gulp) meeeeeee!"

Stacey glanced at the top of the stairs. Margo and Vanessa were standing there solemnly, looking down at their little sister. Stacey said later that that's when she first thought something was really wrong. If the older girls had pulled some sort of prank, they would have been laughing hysterically at the sight of the foam. But they were as somber and silent as rocks.

"Margo? Vanessa?" Stacey said. She steadied Claire and began to lead her upstairs.

"It's not our fault!" Margo cried. "Really."

"Honest," added Vanessa, wide-eyed. "Don't blame us." She was so upset, she forgot to rhyme her words.

Stacey made a huge effort to control her temper. "What happened?" she asked.

Nobody said a word.

"Claire?" Stacey peered into Claire's face, wiping away some foam.

"Shampoo," Claire managed to reply.

"Shampoo? Is that all?" said Stacey, suddenly feeling better. "You guys tried to give your sister a shampoo? Well, what's wrong with that? It was very thoughtful. I just wish you'd asked me first. Come on, Claire. All we have to do is wash it out."

Still the girls remained quiet. Stacey noticed that the foam was unlike any she'd seen before. It was thick, almost as thick as shaving cream, and just slightly blue in color. But Stacey didn't pay any attention to that. She simply drew a bath for Claire, stripped off her clothes, and sat her in the tub. Then she began to rinse the soap off by pouring cupfuls of water over her head.

"Ow! Ow! Owie!" cried Claire.

"What's wrong?" asked Stacey.

"It stings."

"Keep your eyes shut, okay?"

"Okay," replied Claire, "but it still stings."

It wasn't until Stacey had poured twelve cups of water over Claire's head that she began to feel uneasy again. The shampoo wasn't rinsing out.

Stacey dumped another cupful onto Claire. This time she rubbed Claire's hair vigorously. The foam puffed up as if it were alive. It was thicker than ever.

"Margo? Vanessa?" said Stacey.

"Yes?" they whispered. They were sitting squashed together on the toilet, their hands in their laps. They'd watched the rinsing process wordlessly.

"What shampoo did you use on Claire? The baby shampoo?"

Stacey had given Claire several shampoos when she and Mary Anne had gone to Sea City with the Pikes. She had always used Johnson's Baby Shampoo. Nothing like this had ever happened.

"Um, no," replied Vanessa. "We used . . . we used something new."

"What was it?" asked Stacey.

"I don't remember the name."

"Can you show it to me, please?"

Margo and Vanessa looked at each other. Vanessa nodded at her sister. Margo reached behind her and pulled something out of the wastebasket. She handed it to Stacey.

It was a small plastic bottle. And it was empty.

"You guys," said Stacey nervously. "I hope this wasn't your mom's. You didn't use up something of your mom's . . . did you?"

They shook their heads.

Stacey read the label on the front of the bottle. It said:

Trial Size Only
Not for sale
CALLADEW'S PERFECTION SHAMPOO
Concentrated

On the back, the directions cautioned:

Concentrated shampoo — use sparingly.
Pour several drops onto palm of hand.

Rub hands together vigorously to create foam.
Rub foam into hair.
Rinse twice.
Process need not be repeated.

Stacey looked up at the girls. "Where did you get this?" she asked.

"In the mail," Vanessa replied. She didn't look at Stacey. "Mom and Dad always let us have the samples."

"Last week we got two sticks of gum," added Margo.

"And *you* guys ate them," said Claire accusingly from under her cap of foam.

"So this came in the mail today?" said Stacey. Margo and Vanessa nodded.

"I hate to ask, but how much did you use?"

"The whole bottle," said Vanessa. "We felt bad for taking all the gum. So we gave Claire all the shampoo."

"Oh, Vanessa." Stacey was irritated and couldn't hide it. "You're old enough to know you're supposed to read the directions first. Didn't you look at the label?"

Vanessa hung her head. "No," she murmured.

Stacey realized she ought to see what Nicky was up to. She got to her feet. "I want you two to stay here and keep rinsing. I have to check on Nicky. I'll be right back. Be nice to your sister."

Stacey went downstairs, partly to calm down. That, of course, was when she discovered that Nicky was gone. Forty-five minutes later, Claire still had a head of foam, and Nicky still hadn't returned.

Stacey called me. I was at home alone and had been hearing one weird sound after another coming from the secret passage. I was delighted to give Stacey a hand. I couldn't wait to get out of my house.

"Oh, *thank* you for coming!" Stacey exclaimed when I reached the Pikes'. "Mrs. Pike is going to be home in about fifteen minutes, and I have two disasters here. Can you go look for Nicky? I better stay with the mess in the bathroom."

It was getting to be a familiar scene. I walked around our neighborhood calling Nicky at the top of my lungs. He didn't answer. I looked behind bushes and up trees. He was a champion hider.

I had just reached the edge of my property when once again, Nicky appeared suddenly. He was dusty, and a vaguely familiar odor clung to him, but I couldn't quite place it.

"Hi," he said. "Looking for me?" He flashed me a grin, then went on chewing away at an enormous wad of gum.

"Nicky! Where have you been? Stacey was worried."

Nicky wet his hand and rubbed at a scab on his knee. Then he blew a large bubble that popped, leaving wispy pink strings all over his face. But he didn't answer me.

"You are an absolute mess," I told him. "You're filthy."

"Yeah," he said, sounding pleased.

I shook my head. "Come on. I'll walk you back to your house. Your mom'll be home any minute now."

"Okay." Unexpectedly, Nicky slipped his hand into mine as we walked along. It was dirty, sticky, and wet, but I held on to it.

When we reached his front door, I opened it and called inside to Stacey. Then I left. I didn't think it would look good for me to be there when Mrs. Pike returned.

Stacey was relieved to see Nicky, but Vanessa wasn't. She was in a bad mood. Stacey had said that she would have to tell her mother what she and Margo had done.

"Why isn't Nicky in trouble, too?" she demanded.

Before Stacey could answer, Nicky broke in, "Oh, you're just jealous! You wish *you* had a dog friend who could rescue people from avalanches."

"A dog friend! What are you talking about? You don't have any dog friend," scoffed Vanessa.

"Do too!"

"Do not!"

"Can it, you guys!" ordered Stacey.

I wasn't around to hear any of that, but if I had been, it might have helped me out. As it was, an idea was growing in my mind. Just a little one. A sprout. Just enough to make me think I wouldn't have to worry about sounds in the passage again that day.

As it turned out, I was right.

CHAPTER 13

There were no more sounds in the secret passage that afternoon. I even felt brave enough to explore it again. I propped the wall open in my room and entered, carrying a flashlight. I walked purposefully to the spot where I'd found the book the day Mary Anne had been over. I wished I hadn't left it there. I wanted to get a good look at it. But it was gone.

I sighed.

Then I checked out the rest of the passage. The nickel was still gone, the peanut shells were still there, and a crust of bread had turned up. I didn't feel too surprised.

At least — not until I found the key. It was similar to the one I'd found before, but smaller. And a lot older looking. It was shoved into a corner at the bottom of the steps.

It almost ruined my theory.

I left it where it was and tried not to think about it.

I wanted to test my theory, but I didn't have a chance for two whole days. They were the longest days of my life. During that time, the passage was quiet except for very late one night when we had some rain. Then I heard definite moaning coming from the passage. Even though my wall was locked, I grabbed my pillow and blanket and spent the rest of the night on the couch in the living room.

The next day, I had a sitting job at the Pikes'. Mrs. Pike was taking Claire, Margo, and Vanessa to the mall to get their hair cut before school started. (Claire's hair hadn't looked *quite* the same since her sisters had washed it with Calladew's.) Mallory and I were left in charge of Nicky and the triplets.

The afternoon got off to a good start. For once, the triplets allowed Nicky to play with them. The four boys tore around on their driveway, shooting baskets. They'd split into teams — the triplets against Nicky — but Nicky seemed satisfied.

"What should we make for lunch?" I asked Mallory.

It was late for lunch, but Mrs. Pike had had a hectic morning and hadn't gotten around to feeding the kids lunch. She was going to feed the girls at the mall. (That probably happens a lot when you have eight children.)

"Let's do a smorgasbord," said Mallory.

"How?" I asked.

"It's simple. We take everything out of the refrigerator, put it on the table, and let the boys fix whatever they want."

I laughed. "It sounds messy."

"It is," agreed Mallory, "but it's fun. And Mom likes us to use up leftovers."

I looked inside the refrigerator. Then I looked back at Mallory. "Okay," I said. "Let's do it."

We only needed about two minutes to pull everything out of the refrigerator and arrange it on the kitchen table. Then we set out plates, cups, napkins, and forks, and called the boys inside.

"All *right!*" cried Jordan when he got a look at the kitchen.

"Yeah!" exclaimed Nicky. "All *right!* We're having a schmurgerbeard!"

"That's smorgasbord, stupid," said one of the triplets.

"Don't call Nicky stupid," I said.

Nobody even heard me.

Adam was glopping mayonnaise onto a piece of bread.

Byron was digging into the peanut butter with one hand, and eating a dill pickle with the other.

And Jordan was standing at the stove, turning the flame up under a frying pan.

"Jordan! What are you doing?" I cried.

"Making fried baloney."

"Well, let me do that."

I was beginning to think that the schmurgerbeard hadn't been such a good idea. "Does anyone else want fried baloney?" I asked.

"I want fried peanut butter and jelly," replied Byron.

"I want a fried egg," replied Adam.

"I want fried barf," replied Nicky.

"Ha, ha. So funny I forgot to laugh," said Jordan.

The triplets looked at each other, smirking.

"Hey, Nicky," said Adam, "say Mark Twain's initials and point to your head."

"Oh, simple," said Nicky. He pointed to his left ear. "M.T."

The triplets doubled over with laughter.

"M.T. Empty!" hooted Adam. "Get it? You've got nothing in your head, Nicky. Not one little brain. It's empty!"

"Ha, ha. So funny I forgot to laugh," said Nicky.

I thought his comeback was pretty good, considering, but the triplets barely heard him.

"Come on now," I said. "Who wants fried what?"

After much debate, I made fried baloney for Jordan and Adam, and a fried peanut butter and jelly sandwich for Byron. Nicky said he wasn't hungry, but finally fixed himself a potato chip and banana sandwich. I started to say something to him about that, and then remembered that the Pike kids are allowed to eat whatever they want (within reason). Mallory made tuna-fish sandwiches for the two of us.

We carried our lunches to the table on the sun porch. Everything was peaceful until the very end of the meal. Nicky, who had been silent since the Mark Twain incident, stood up and stacked his glass on his plate.

"Here, Nicky. You want the rest of this cupcake?" asked Adam, holding out half of a gooey chocolate concoction. He must have been having an attack of conscience.

"Sure," said Nicky, flattered. He set his plate down.

As he did so, Adam reached behind him and pulled his chair out from under him.

Nicky sat down hard on the floor.

"Adam!" I shouted. The triplets knew I was angry, but they couldn't help laughing silently, their faces turning red and their eyes filling with tears of laughter.

Nicky sat on the floor for a moment, looking surprised. Then he scrambled to his feet and ran off the porch. A second later, the front door slammed.

I counted to ten before I opened my mouth. Then I said very quietly, "You three are in major trouble."

The laughter stopped.

"You've been rotten to Nicky today. Really rotten. I'm going to have to tell your mother about this."

"Aw —" began Jordan.

"Nope!" I cried. "I don't want to hear a word about it. Right now I'm going to look for your brother. Mallory will be in charge. I want to see the porch and the kitchen sparkling by the time I get back. And if you give Mallory any trouble, your mother will hear about that, too."

I marched out of the Pikes' house. The triplets had rarely seen me angry. That's because I rarely *get* angry. Sometimes I pout or feel cross, but I don't often scold. And I had never scolded the

Pikes. I felt kind of bad about it, but the triplets had really been mean to Nicky. I hoped Mallory knew I wasn't angry at her. Oh, well. I'd straighten everything out when I got back.

As I ran down the street, my anger began to turn to excitement. I realized that I was finally going to have the chance to test my theory!

I didn't bother to call for Nicky. I ran right to my own house, darted across the lawn, around to the back, and into the barn. I paused to let my eyes adjust to the dim light.

Just as I expected, the bale of hay that Mom had shoved over the trapdoor had been moved aside. In fact, the trapdoor itself was open. I drew in my breath and stepped boldly down the ladder.

"Nicky?" I called, but my voice was no higher than a whisper.

I jumped down the last two rungs.

"Nicky?"

That was when I realized I didn't even have a flashlight. If Nicky wasn't going to answer me, then I'd have to go after him. I ran into our kitchen, found a flashlight, and ran back out to the barn.

"Nicky!" I called again as I lowered myself through the trapdoor.

I thought I could hear heavy breathing, but when I shined the light around I saw nothing but darkness. An awful thought struck me then: What if I was wrong? What if it wasn't Nicky in the passage? What if it was *Jared*?

The thought scared me so that I climbed all the way back up the ladder and sat down on the bale of hay.

I considered calling my mother.

I considered calling Mary Anne.

I considered calling the police.

But I didn't call any of them. I wanted to solve the mystery. I turned over the evidence and the clues I had gathered:

I had found some very old things in the secret passage. They looked like they had been there for years. I had kept them.

I had seen some things in the passage that had later disappeared.

Some other things had appeared in the passage and stayed there (like the peanut shells and the bread crust).

I had heard *tons* of weird noises coming from the passage. I'd heard a lot of them during the day, but I'd heard some of them in the dead of night.

Nicky might be in the passage now . . . and he might not. I decided to take a chance.

I eased myself through the trapdoor again and jumped onto the dirt floor. Now *there* was something that had always bothered me. Why was the dirt floor so hard-packed? Simple, I answered myself. Because it had been walked on a lot, even before I found it. Someone had been using the passage frequently — and it wasn't Jared, since ghosts don't weigh anything.

I took a deep breath and marched forward.

"Nicky!" I called. "I'm coming after you right now."

I heard footsteps then, far down the passage. With a pounding heart, I followed them.

CHAPTER 14

The footsteps began to run, and I ran after them.

The footsteps thumped up the stairs. I thumped after them.

Then I turned the corner and shined the light ahead of me to the end of the passage.

Crouched in one corner was a small figure.

"Nicky!" I exclaimed. "So it *is* you, after all."

Nicky didn't answer. I ran to him.

"Nicky?" I said again.

"Oh, *Dawn*!" he burst out. "Why'd you have to find me?"

"Is this your secret place? Is this where you go when you disappear?"

He nodded. "Well, not *right* here. Usually I stop when I get to the stairs. I mean, this is your house. I didn't want to trespass or anything. . . . We are somewhere inside your house, aren't we?"

"Yeah. You don't know where the passage ends up?"

"Just in this dead end, I thought."

"Nope. Not quite. I'll show you." I was pretty sure my wall was unlocked, so I released the catch.

Nicky watched wide-eyed as the wall in front of him began to move back. Through the opening, my bedspread appeared, then the dresser, the curtains, and the armchair. Nicky found himself practically in my room.

He stood up and peered inside, then looked back at me. "Whoa . . ."

"My bedroom," I said. "Come on in."

Nicky followed me inside. I showed him how the wall closed up.

"You can't even see a crack!" he exclaimed.

"I know," I said. "I looked for a secret passage in the house forever, and I never found this."

"I found the other end really easily," said Nicky in a small voice.

Nicky looked completely out of place in my bedroom. He was dirty and dusty (so was I, for that matter, but only slightly), he had chocolate cake mashed on one arm, and his cheeks were streaked with tears. Messy as he was, he was sitting on my clean white bedspread. I didn't care, though.

"You want to tell me about it, Nicky?" He shrugged.

"How'd you find the other end?"

Nicky sighed. "One day Adam kept teasing me about this book I was reading. So I took the book —"

"Was it *Great Dog Tales*?" I interrupted.

"How did you know?"

"I saw it in the passage once. You must have left it there."

"Oh. Well, anyway, I took the book and I ran away. I didn't break the two-block rule, Dawn. I swear I didn't. The back of your barn is exactly two blocks from the front of our house. I didn't know if any of you guys were home, but I didn't think you used the barn, so I snuck inside. It's so quiet in there."

"I know."

"And I was looking for a place to read when I found the trapdoor instead. I opened it up and climbed down the ladder. And that's how I found the passage."

"And you started coming back?" I prompted him.

"Yeah. I kept a flashlight buried under some hay near the trapdoor, and I could go in the passage and think of mean things to say to the triplets or read or look at my coin collection."

"Your coin collection? Oh, boy. I have about a million questions to ask you."

"You do?" Nicky looked puzzled.

"Yeah. See, I thought the secret passage had a ghost."

"A *ghost*?" Nicky shrieked. "I've been going some place where there's a ghost?"

"No, silly," I said. "*You* were the ghost."

"Oh."

"I mean, I *think* you were. Do you have a Buffalo nickel in your coin collection?"

"Yeah."

"Did you lose it?"

"Yup. But I found it again."

"I found it, too." I told him about the stormy night and the Trip-Man.

Nicky laughed.

"Did you ever bring snacks over here?" I asked.

"Lots of times," he replied. "Once, I even brought an ice-cream cone. The Frosty Treats truck drove by just as I got to the barn. So I bought a cone. It was called a Fancy Old-Fashioned Ice-Cream Parlour Cone and it cost a whole dollar."

"I found the end of the cone," I told him. "And some other things."

"Sorry," said Nicky. "I guess I didn't clean up too good."

"Too *well*," I corrected him, "and you cleaned up just fine. I only found a couple of things. I thought the ghost had a sweet tooth."

Nicky giggled. "I was here just this morning eating peanuts. That's why I wasn't hungry for lunch," he confessed. "You know," he went on, "now that I know you used the passage, you answered a question for me."

"What's that?"

"I used to see these old things in the passage."

"A key, a buckle, and a button," I said.

"Yes. Did you take them? I couldn't figure out what happened to them."

"I took them," I said. "They're in my drawer. Where'd you get that other key, though?"

"What other key?"

"The *really* old one. The one at the bottom of the steps."

"I've never seen another key," replied Nicky. "So it can't be mine."

"Are you *sure*? I know it wasn't there a few days ago."

"It isn't mine. Honest."

"I believe you," I said, my skin crawling. If the key wasn't mine and it wasn't Nicky's, whose was it? Jared's?

"What's the matter, Dawn?" asked Nicky.

I shivered. "Nothing . . . I'm sorry I ruined your secret hiding place."

"That's okay," replied Nicky, but he didn't sound as if it were okay at all.

"I don't mind that you were coming to our passageway, Nicky," I told him. "I really don't. But you do know that it wasn't *quite* right, don't you?"

Nicky looked worried. "What?"

"Well," I said, "technically, I guess you were trespassing, but that's not what I mean. What I mean is that, for one thing, you scared me. You made noises when you were in the passage. That was another reason I thought we had a ghost."

"I didn't mean to make any noise."

"I know you didn't. By the way, did you ever hide in the passage at night?"

"At night?" exclaimed Nicky. "No way."

"I didn't think so." I tried not to start shivering again. Who had been moaning and creaking around the passage during the night-time thunderstorms?

"I'm sorry I scared you," said Nicky.

"It's okay. Really. Let's go back to your house. Your mom's going to be home soon."

"All right." Nicky looked as if I were going to lead him into a pit of vipers.

We left my house and headed back to the Pikes'. "Another thing," I added as we walked along. "I don't know how safe the passage is. Those stairs are old. So's the trapdoor." Nicky nodded glumly.

"Last thing," I said. "When your mother made up the two-block rule for you, I don't think she meant for you to go someplace where no one could find you. That's just not a good idea. Okay?"

"Okay."

I took Nicky's hand. "Hey," I said. "Look at that. Your mom beat us home. Let's go tell her about your adventure."

Mrs. Pike had been surprised, to say the least, when she had come back and found that I wasn't there, but I explained the whole story to her, including the triplets' pranks. Mallory, luckily, had done just fine with her brothers. While I was chasing after Nicky, she had gotten them to clean up lunch and then had settled them into a game of Monopoly. They were extremely quiet and well-behaved when I returned. I was really impressed with Mallory.

Mrs. Pike and Nicky and I had a talk before I went home.

"I *need* a hideout," Nicky said, sounding the way people do when they talk about very important things, like food or money.

"I understand that, sweetie," said Mrs. Pike.

"Well," I spoke up, "I'll have to check with my mom, but it's all right with me if Nicky comes back to our passage."

"It's all right with me, too," said Mrs. Pike after a moment, "as long as you tell an adult where you're going first, Nicky. And maybe someone should check the condition of the passage."

"Yippee!" cried Nicky. "I just hope the triplets don't start going there."

"Believe me, they won't," said his mother.

"How do you know?" asked Nicky.

"Because I'm about to have a little talk with them."

Nicky turned to me, all smiles. "You," he said, "are my favorite baby-sitter in the whole wide world."

CHAPTER 15

"So what movie do you guys want to watch?" I asked.

"*Ghostbusters*," said Kristy.

"*Star Wars*," said Claudia.

"*Mary Poppins*," said Stacey.

"*Sixteen Candles*," said Mary Anne.

"And I want to watch *The Parent Trap*," I said, looking woefully at the VCR.

It was Saturday night. The members of the Baby-sitters Club were crowded into my living room. We were having a slumber party. Upstairs, sleeping bags were spread over every inch of the floor of my bedroom. The bathroom was a disaster area. It looked like a makeup tornado had ripped through it. (But our faces looked great. Stacey and Claudia had practiced on all of us.) We had finished supper, and now we were settling in for a long night in front of the VCR.

"Maybe we could watch all of them," suggested Claudia.

"Well," I said, "let's see. If each one is about two hours long —"

"*Mary Poppins* is longer, I think," said Stacey.

"But *Sixteen Candles* is shorter," Mary Anne pointed out.

"An *average*," I said. "Just an *average*. What I was going to say is that that comes to about ten hours of movies. It's nine o'clock now. That would take us right up to seven in the morning."

We laughed.

"Let's pick two," I said. "We'll vote on them."

Everyone voted for the movie she had suggested plus one other. We ended up with a five-way tie. In the end, Kristy drew two of the movies out of a hat. (After all, she's the club president.) The winners were *Sixteen Candles* and *Ghostbusters*.

"Mary Anne was jubilant. She'd brought two copies of *Sixteen* magazine with her, and there was an article about Cam Geary, the love of her life, in it. Cam Geary and *Sixteen Candles* created a really prime evening for Mary Anne.

We watched *Ghostbusters* first. Much as I like *The Parent Trap*, I have to admit that *Ghostbusters* is pretty funny. My favorite part is when that giant marshmallow guy bursts. I think it's Kristy's favorite part, too. As soon as he exploded, she said, "I'm starving! Let's toast marshmallows, Dawn. Or make s'mores."

"Kristy, we don't have stuff like that at my house. It's junk food."

Kristy and Claudia glanced at each other. "Be right back," they said, and ran upstairs.

They returned holding a bag of marshmallows, some candy bars, a box of graham crackers, a bag of potato chips, a supply of M&M's and some crackers.

"Pig-out time!" said Kristy. "I hope you don't mind, Dawn. We can't have a slumber party without this stuff. It isn't normal." She tossed the crackers to me. "Those are for you and Stacey," she said.

Stacey and I looked at each other. We made faces. But then we couldn't help laughing. It *was* kind of funny.

"Where'd you get all that?" I asked.

"Mary Anne and Claudia and I bought it this afternoon," said Kristy. "We thought it might be a good idea to come prepared. Don't worry, we paid for it ourselves, not out of the club treasury."

Kristy pressed the pause button on the VCR and Bill Murray froze in action. "Quick! Let's make the s'mores before the movie comes back on!" she cried.

Kristy grabbed the marshmallows.

Mary Anne grabbed the graham crackers.

Claudia grabbed the Hershey's bars.

The three of them tore off, leaving Stacey and me behind in a trail of dust (so to speak).

"Boy," I said, "Just because we don't eat that junk of theirs."

"Really," agreed Stacey. "I feel like a leper."

"*I* feel like a nerd."

"We shouldn't, though," said Stacey. "They're the ones who're going to end up with pimples."

I giggled. "Let's get them."

"Pimples?"

"*No!* I mean, I have a plan. We'll get back at Kristy and the others. Remember our search for a secret passage?"

Stacey nodded. "Well, I found one."

"No."

"Yup."

"Honest?"

"Cross my heart. So here's what I think we should do."

I leaned over and began to whisper to Stacey. We had just finished planning, when Kristy and Claudia and Mary Anne came back. They were eating these gooey concoctions and had chocolate all over their fingers. Every time they took a bite of their s'mores, the melted marshmallow would string out between their mouths and hands.

Stacey and I had a hard time keeping straight faces. Somehow, though, we made it through the rest of *Ghostbusters* without giving anything away.

As soon as the movie was over, Mary Anne dove for the rewind button. "Time for *Sixteen Candles*," she said.

"Why don't we watch it later?" I suggested casually. "Wouldn't it be fun to watch it at, like, one or two this morning?"

"Yeah!" said Kristy enthusiastically. (I knew I could count on her. She loves to stay up late.)

Mary Anne looked disappointed, but she didn't want to argue with the rest of us.

"Let's go up to my room for awhile," I said. "You know Cam Geary's girlfriend, Mary Anne?"

"Corrie Lalique?" she replied immediately.

"Yeah. I bet with a little more make-up I could make you look just like her."

"Really? Oh, hey, great!"

Mary Anne was the first one upstairs. The rest of us followed. After we'd worked on her for a while, I said, "Boy, am I thirsty."

"Oh, me, too," chimed in Stacey.

"So am I," said the others at once. (It figured, after all that sugar.)

"I'll go get some sodas," I said. "Come with me, Stace. Okay?"

"You have soda?" asked Claudia skeptically. "Or do you mean Perrier or sparkling, salt-less mineral water from an artesian well or something?"

I tried not to sound sarcastic. "Yes, we have soda. Real soda. Mom bought it for the party. One hundred percent sugar."

"Good," said Claudia, not cracking a smile.

"Come on, Stace."

We ran downstairs. It was time to put our plan into action.

"What's your mom going to say?" asked Stacey nervously.

"Nothing," I replied. "I warned her when we went upstairs before. And Jeff's already in bed, so we don't have to worry about him. Unless the screaming gets too loud."

Stacey laughed. She and I stopped in the kitchen for flashlights. We turned them on, aimed the beams out the back door, and crept outside as quietly as possible. I led Stacey into the barn, shoved aside the bale of hay, and showed her the trapdoor. We lowered ourselves down the ladder.

"I don't believe it," whispered Stacey slowly. "This is awesome."

"Are you scared?" I asked. I hadn't told her about Jared Mullray.

"Not really. I'm not wild about the dark, but . . . let's go!"

When we'd climbed the flight of stairs and turned the corner, we paused to listen. Very faintly we could hear the voices of Mary Anne, Claudia, and Kristy.

"Now?" whispered Stacey.

"Now," I replied. "And when they've had enough, just follow me."

"Okay."

Stacey rapped lightly on a wall of the passage. I scratched on another.

We paused. The girls were still talking.

"Louder," I whispered.

We rapped and scratched more loudly. The talking stopped, then started again.

"Closer," I suggested.

We crept down the passage. Our friends' voices grew louder.

Rap, rap. Rap, rap, rap.
Scritch, scratch.

Then I distinctly heard Claudia say, "Did you guys hear something?"

Stacey and I tried not to laugh.

"Try wailing," said Stacey.

"Oooooo-eeeeee. Heeeeeelp meeeeee!" I wailed.

"Whoooooo-oooooo-eeeeee. I caaaaaannot reeeeeeest!" cried Stacey. It was a brilliant choice of words.

"Aughh!" cried one of the girls in my room, but I couldn't tell which one.

"Oh, no! It's Jared! It's the ghost of the secret passage!" yelped Mary Anne.

"What?" asked Kristy. "What ghost?" (She was probably thinking of old Ben Brewer.)

"What secret passage?" added Claudia.

Rap, rap, rap. Bang, bang, bang.

I noticed a pipe, and tapped my flashlight on it. *Clink, clink.*

"Aughh!" The shrieking in the bedroom sounded more frightened. We heard a crash.

"I think that's enough," I said. "Come on."

I dashed to the end of the passage and released the catch. The wall of my bedroom slowly opened inward.

Stacey and I were looking in on a disaster area. A chair had been knocked over. A container of eye shadow was on the rug. The sleeping bags were rumpled, as if they'd been run over by galloping horses. And Kristy, Claudia, and Mary Anne were huddled on my bed.

"I told you it was the ghost," Mary Anne was moaning.

Then Stacey and I stuck our heads in the room. When Kristy saw us, she fell off the bed.

There was a moment of silence.

"You!" shrieked Mary Anne. "It was *you*!"

"You stinkers!" Kristy exploded, rubbing one elbow. She got to her feet.

Stacey and I laughed so hard that tears ran down our faces. We couldn't speak. We dropped our flashlights on the bed and I closed the wall behind me.

"You found a secret passage," was all Claudia could say. "How?"

I explained. I told my friends the story — Nicky, Jared Mullray, the nickel. But I left out the parts about the small key, and the nighttime noises.

"Oh, let's go inside!" exclaimed Claudia.

"Please? I've never been in a true secret passage. And I've always wanted to have the chance."

"Okay," I said. "Sure. We'll all go."

I was reaching for the wall when . . .

Rap, rap, rap.

It had come from the passage. Wide-eyed, I whirled around. All four of my friends were behind me. I dashed out of my room. Mom was reading in bed. Jeff was sound asleep.

I looked at my watch. Almost one o'clock. It wasn't Nicky.

In a panic, I went back to my room and fastened the lock on the wall. "Come on, you guys. Bring your sleeping bags. We'll stay in the living room tonight."

And we did. But it took us forever to fall asleep.

Did my secret passage have a ghost? I hoped I'd never find out.

The next morning dawned clear and sunny. I was awakened by the sound of a catbird outside the open window. The scent of newly mown grass drifted in and mingled with the smells of toast and eggs coming from the kitchen.

I rolled over sleepily.

"Hi," whispered Kristy from her sleeping bag.

"Morning," I replied.

Stacey, Claudia, and Mary Anne were still asleep.

"You know," said Kristy, "we only have a few,

and I mean a *few*, more days until school starts again."

I made a face. "I know."

"We better use them wisely."

"What do you mean?"

"Well, we've just had a slumber party. While there's still time, we better try to cram in a few more good activities. Like swimming."

"Going to the movies," I said.

"Having a gossip-fest."

"Lying around in the sun reading magazines."

"Playing tennis."

"Swinging on the rope in the barn."

"Going to the mall," murmured Stacey, without bothering to open her eyes.

"Making s'more s'mores," mumbled Claudia.

"Having a cookout," said Mary Anne, only her face was buried in her pillow and it sounded like she said, "Havee a fuh-fow."

"Boy," I exclaimed, "we've got a lot to do and very little time. We better get going!"

I felt excited, exhilarated. With friends like these, and so much to look forward to, who could worry about a crazy two hundred-year-old guy named Jared Mullray? Not me!

About the Author

Ann M. Martin's The Baby-sitters Club has sold over 180 million copies and inspired a generation of young readers. Her novels include the Newbery Honor Book *A Corner of the Universe*, *A Dog's Life*, and the Main Street series. She lives in upstate New York.

Keep reading for a sneak peek at the next book
from The Baby-sitters Club!

Logan Likes Mary Anne!

Claudia and Stacey and I walked to school together the next morning, since the three of us live in the same neighborhood. It was the first time ever that Kristy and I hadn't walked off together on day number one of a school year. But Kristy had to take the bus from her new home. (Dawn, who lived not too far away, often took a different route to school, and sometimes her mother drove her there on her way to work.)

I was all set for eighth grade. My brand-new binder was filled with fresh paper; I had inserted neatly labeled dividers, one for each subject, among the paper; and a pencil case containing pens, pencils, an eraser, a ruler, and a pack of gum was clipped to the inside front cover. My lunch money was in my purse, the photo of Cam Geary was folded and ready to be displayed in my locker. (That was what the gum was for. You're not allowed to tape things up in the lockers of Stoneybrook Middle School, so a lot of kids get around that rule by sticking them up with bits of freshly chewed gum.) The only thing about me not ready for eighth grade was my age. I had the latest birthday of all my friends and wouldn't turn thirteen for several more weeks.

Starting eighth grade seemed like a breeze to me. I'd been a chicken when we'd begun sixth grade, and I was going to be one of the youngest kids in the school. I hadn't been much better when we'd started seventh grade the year before. But now I felt like king of the hill. The eighth-graders were the oldest kids in school. We would get to do special things during the year. We would have a real graduation ceremony in June. After that, we would go on to the high school. Pretty important stuff.

But I couldn't decide whether to be excited or disappointed about the beginning of school. When we reached Stoneybrook Middle School, Stacey and Claudia and I just looked at each other.

Finally Claudia said, "Well, good-bye, summer."

Then Stacey started speaking in her Porky Pig voice. "Th-th-th-th-th-th-th-that's all, folks!" she exclaimed, waving her hand.

Claudia and I laughed. Then we split up. There were three eighth-grade homerooms, and we were each in a different one. I went to my locker first, working half a piece of gum around in my mouth on the way. "Hello, old locker," I said to myself as I spun the dial on number 132. I opened the door. This was the only morning all year that my locker would be absolutely empty when I opened it. I pulled the poster of Cam Geary out of my notebook and set the notebook and my purse on the shelf of the locker. Then I unfolded the poster. I took the gum out of my mouth, checked the hall for teachers, and divided the gum into four bits, one for each corner. There. The poster stayed up nicely. I could look at Cam's gorgeous face all year.

I picked up my notebook and purse, closed my locker, and made my way upstairs. The hallways were already pretty crowded. Kids showed up early (or at least on time) for the first day of school.

My homeroom was 216, about as far from my locker as you could get. I entered it breathlessly, then slowed down. Suddenly I felt shy. Dawn was supposed to be in my homeroom, but she wasn't there yet. The room was full of kids I didn't know very well. And where was I supposed to sit? The teacher, Mr. Blake, was at his desk, but he looked busy. Had he planned on assigned seating? Could we sit wherever we wanted? I stood awkwardly by the door.

"Mary Anne! Hi!" said someone behind me.

Oh, thank goodness. It was Dawn.

I spun around. "Hi! I just got here," I told her.

Mr. Blake still wasn't paying attention to the kids gathering in his room.

"Let's sit in back," suggested Dawn.

So we did. We watched Erica Blumberg and Shawna Riverson compare tans. We watched a new kid creep into the room and choose a seat in a corner without looking at anyone. We watched three boys whisper about Erica and Shawna.

At last the teacher stood up. "Roll call," he announced, and the first day of school was truly underway.

This was my morning schedule:

First period – English
Second period – math
Third period – gym (yuck)
Fourth period – social studies
Fifth period – lunch

My afternoon schedule wasn't so bad: science, study hall, and French class. But I thought my morning schedule was sort of heavy, and by lunchtime I was starved.

Kristy (who was in my social studies class) raced down to the cafeteria with me. We claimed the table we used to sit at last year with Dawn and some of our other friends. (Stacey and Claudia usually sat with their own group of kids.) In a moment Dawn showed up. She settled down and opened her bag lunch while Kristy and I went through the lunch line. Last year we'd brought our lunches, too. This year we'd decided brown bags looked babyish.

When we returned to the table with our trays, we were surprised to find Stacey and Claudia there with *their* trays. Since when had they decided to eat with us? We were good friends, but last year they always thought they were so much more sophisticated than we were. They liked to talk about boys and movie stars and who was going out with whom. . . . Had Stacey and Claudia changed, or had Kristy and Dawn and I? I almost said something, but I decided not to. I knew we were all thinking that eating together was different and nice — and also that we weren't going to mention that it was happening.

I opened my milk carton, put my napkin in my lap, and took a good long look at the Stoneybrook Middle School hot lunch.

"What *is* this?" I asked the others.

"Noodles," replied Kristy.

"No, it's poison," said Dawn, who, as usual, was eating a health-food lunch — a container of strawberries, a yogurt with granola mixed in, some dried apple slices, and something I couldn't identify.

"I don't see any noodles here," I said. "Only glue."

"According to the menu, that glue is mushroom and cream sauce," said Claudia.

"Ew," I replied.

"So," said Dawn, "how was everybody's first morning back at school?"

"Fine, Mommy," answered Stacey.

Dawn giggled.

"I have third-period gym with Mrs. Rosenauer," I said. "I hate field hockey, I hate Mrs. Rosenauer, and I hate smelling like gym class for the next five periods. . . . Do I smell like gym class?" I leaned toward Kristy.

She pulled back. "*I'm* not going to smell you. . . . Hey, I just figured something out. You know what the mushroom sauce tastes like? It tastes like a dirty sock that's been left out in the rain and then hidden in a dark closet for three weeks."

The rest of us couldn't decide whether to gag or giggle.

Maybe this was why Claudia and Stacey didn't sit with us last year. I changed the subject. "I put the poster of Cam Geary up in my locker this morning," I announced. "I'm going to leave him there all year."

"I want to find a picture of Max Morrison," said Claudia. "That's who I'd like in my locker."

"The boy from 'Out of This World'?" asked Stacey.

Claudia nodded.

I absolutely couldn't eat another bite of the noodles, not after what Kristy had said about the sauce. I gazed around the cafeteria. I saw Trevor Sandbourne, one of Claudia's old boyfriends from last year. I saw the Shillaber twins, who used to sit with Kristy and Dawn and me. They were sitting with the only set of boy twins in school. (For a moment, I thought I had double vision.) I saw Erica and Shawna from homeroom. And then I saw Cam Geary.

I nearly spit out a mouthful of milk.

"Stacey!" I whispered after I'd managed to swallow. "Cam Geary goes to our school! Look!"

All my friends turned to look. "Where? Where?"

"That boy?" said Stacey, smiling. "That's not Cam Geary. That's Logan Bruno. He's new this year. He's in my homeroom and my English class. I talked to him during homeroom. He used to live in Louisville, Kentucky. He has a southern accent."

I didn't care what he sounded like. He was the cutest boy I'd ever seen. He looked exactly like Cam Geary. I was in love with him. And because Stacey already knew so much about him, I was jealous of her. What a way to start the year.

The next day, Friday, was the second day of school, and the end of the first "week" of school. And that night, the members of the Baby-sitters Club held the first meeting of eighth grade. Every last one of us just barely made the meeting on time. Claudia had been working on an art project at school (she loves art and is terrific at it), Dawn had been baby-sitting for the Pikes, Stacey had been at school at a meeting of the dance committee, of which she's vice-president, Kristy had had to wait for Charlie to get home from football practice before he could drive her to the meeting, and I'd been trying to get my weekend homework done before the weekend.

The five of us turned up at five-thirty on the nose, and the phone was ringing as we reached Claudia's room. Dawn grabbed for it, while I tried to find the club record book. Everything was in chaos.

"I love it!" said Kristy when we had settled down.

"You love what?" asked Claudia.

"The excitement, the fast pace."

"You should move to New York," said Stacey.

"No, I'm serious. When things get hectic like this, I get all sorts of great ideas. Summertime is too slow."

"What kinds of great ideas do you get?" asked Dawn, who doesn't know Kristy quite the way the rest of us do. I was pretty sure that

Kristy's ideas were going to lead to extra work for the club.

I was right.

"Did you notice the sign in school today?" asked Kristy.

"Kristy, there must have been three thousand signs," replied Claudia. "I saw one for the Remember September Dance, one for the Chess Club, one for cheerleader tryouts, one for class elections —"

"This sign," Kristy interrupted, "was for the PTA. There's going to be a PTA meeting at Stoneybrook Middle School in a few days."

"So?" said Stacey. "PTA stands for Parent Teacher Association. We're kids. It doesn't concern us."

"Oh, yes it does," replied Kristy, "because where there are *parents* there are *children*, and where there are children, there are parents needing babysitters — *us*. That's where we come in."

"*Oh*," I said knowingly. Kristy is so smart. She's such a good businesswoman. That's why she's the president of our club. "More advertising?" I asked.

"Right," replied Kristy.

The phone rang again then, and we stopped to

take another job. When we were finished, Kristy continued. "We've got to advertise in school. We'll put up posters where the parents will see them when they come for the meeting."

"Maybe," added Dawn, "we could make up some more fliers and figure out some way for the parents to get them at the meeting. I think it's always better if people have something they can take with them. You know, something to put up on their refrigerator or by their phone."

"Terrific idea," said Kristy, who usually isn't too generous with her praise.

Dawn beamed.

"There's something else," Kristy went on after we'd lined up jobs with the Marshalls and the Perkinses. "When we started this club, it was so that we could baby-sit in our neighborhood, and the four of us —" (Kristy pointed to herself, Claudia, Stacey, and me) "— all lived in the same neighborhood. Then Dawn joined the club, and we found some new clients in her neighborhood. Now *I've* moved, but I, um, I — I haven't, um . . ."

It was no secret that Kristy had resented moving out of the Thomases' comfortable old split-level and across town to Watson's mansion in his wealthy neighborhood. Of course she liked having a big room with a queen-sized bed and getting treats and being able to have lots of new clothes and stuff. But she'd been living over there for about two months and hadn't made any effort to get to know the people in her new neighborhood. Her brothers had made an effort, and so had her mother, but Kristy claimed that the kids her age were snobs. She and the Thomases' old collie, Louie, kept pretty much to themselves.

I tried to help her through her embarrassment. "It would be good business sense," I pointed out, "to advertise where you live. We should be leaving fliers in the mailboxes over on Edgerstoune Drive and Green House Drive and Bissell Lane."

"And Haslet Avenue and Ober Road, too," said Claudia.

"Right," said Kristy, looking relieved. "After all, I know Linny and Hannie Papadakis — they're friends of David Michael and Karen. They must need a sitter every now and then. And there are probably plenty of other little kids, too."

"And," said Stacey, adding the one thing the rest of us didn't have the nerve to say, "it might be a good way for you to meet people over there."

Kristy scowled. "Oh, right. All those snobs."

"Kristy, they can't *all* be snobs," said Dawn.

"The ones I met were snobs," Kristy said defiantly. "But what does it matter? We might get some new business."

"Well," I said, "can your mom do some more Xeroxing for us?"

Kristy's mother (who used to be Mrs. Thomas and is now Mrs. Brewer) usually takes one of our fliers to her office and Xeroxes it on the machine there when we need more copies. The machine is so fancy, the fliers almost look as if they'd been printed.

"Sure," replied Kristy, "only this time we'll have to give her some money for the Xerox paper. We've used an awful lot of it. What's in the treasury, Stacey?"

Stacey dumped out the contents of a manila envelope. The money in it is our club dues. We each get to keep anything we earn baby-sitting (we don't try to divide it), but we contribute weekly dues of a dollar apiece to the club. The money pays Charlie for driving Kristy to club meetings and buys any supplies we might need.

"We've got a little over fifteen dollars," said our treasurer.

"Well, I don't know how much Xerox paper costs," said Kristy, "but it's only paper. How many pieces do you think we'll need?"

"A hundred?" I guessed. "A hundred and fifty?"

Kristy took eight dollars out of the treasury. "I'll bring back the change," she said. She looked at her watch. "Boy, only ten more minutes left. This meeting sure went fast."

"We couldn't come early and we can't leave late," said Dawn. "Summer's over."

There was a moment of silence. Even the phone didn't ring.

"I found a picture of Max Morrison," Claudia said finally. "It was in *People* magazine. I'm going to bring it to school on Monday."

"Where is it now?" asked Stacey.

"Here." Claudia took it out of her desk drawer and handed it to Stacey.

"Look at his eyes," said Stacey with a sigh.

"No one's eyes are more amazing than Cam's," I said. "Except maybe Logan Bruno's." I'd seen Logan several more times since lunch the day before. Each time I'd thought he was Cam Geary at first. I wished I'd had an excuse to talk to him, but there was none. We didn't have any classes together, so of course he didn't know who I was.

"Logan Bruno?" Claudia repeated sharply. "Hey, you don't . . . you do! I think you like him, Mary Anne!"

Luckily, I was saved by the ringing of the telephone. I took the call myself, and Stacey ended up with a job at the Newtons'.

By the time I had called Mrs. Newton back and noted the job in our appointment book, my friends were on to another subject.

"Kara Mauricio got a bra yesterday," said Dawn.

I could feel myself blushing. I cleared my throat. "I, um, I, um, I, um —"

"Spit it out, Mary Anne," said Kristy.

"I, um, got a bra yesterday."

"You *did*?" Kristy squeaked.

I nodded. "Dad came home early. He took me to the department store and a saleswoman helped me."

"Was it *awfully* embarrassing?" asked Dawn. "At least my mother helped me get my first one. She kept the saleswomen away."

Kristy was gaping at me. We've both always been as flat as pancakes, but I'd begun to grow a little over the summer. Kristy must have felt left out. She was the only one of us who didn't wear a bra now.

But suddenly she was all business again. She doesn't like us to get off the subject of the club for *too* long during meetings. "Let's try to get these fliers out next week. Business will really be booming. Who can help me distribute them?"

We looked at our schedules. A few minutes later, the meeting was over. Little did we know what we were getting ourselves into.

Want more baby-sitting?

Don't miss any of the books in the Baby-sitters Club series by Ann M. Martin—available as ebooks